Captain Tweakerbeak's Revenge

Also by Charles Haddad

Meet Calliope Day

A CALLIOPE DAY ADVENTURE

Captain Tweakerbeak's Revenge

Charles Haddad

Illustrated by Steve Pica

Delacorte Press

Published by
Delacorte Press
an imprint of
Random House Children's Books
a division of Random House, Inc.
1540 Broadway
New York, New York 10036

Visit us on the Web! www.randomhouse.com/kids
Educators and librarians, for a variety of teaching tools,
visit us at www.randomhouse.com/teachers

Library of Congress Cataloging-in-Publication Data
Haddad, Charles (Charles Harold)
    Captain Tweakerbeak's revenge : a Calliope Day adventure /
by Charles Haddad ; illustrated by Steve Pica.
        p.   cm.
    Summary: When mischievous nine-year-old Calliope Day
talks her rich new friend into bringing Captain Tweakerbeak
the parrot to school for a prank, the results are so hilarious
Calliope decides to keep the bird for herself.
    ISBN 0-385-32712-9
    [1. Parrots—Fiction. 2. Schools—Fiction. 3. Friendships—
Fiction. 4. Wealth—Fiction. 5. Humorous stories.] I. Pica,
Steve, ill. II. Title.
PZ7.H1163 Cap 2001
[Fic]—dc21
                                                  00-045173

The text of this book is set in 12-point New Baskerville.
Manufactured in the United States of America
June 2001
10 9 8 7 6 5 4 3 2 1
BVG

Little Miss Prissy Toes

Oh, brother, groaned Calliope Day. Look who her fourth-grade teacher had picked today to ump the kickball game at recess. Little Miss Prissy Toes herself, also known as Noreen Catherwood. It was bad enough that Calliope had to sit next to her in class. But to have to listen to her be umpire was too much.

Calliope sat cross-legged in the thinning grass alongside the kickball diamond. Twisting the untied lace of one of her red Keds, she eyed Noreen while awaiting her turn up at the plate.

Noreen stood behind the pitcher's mound in her shiny black shoes and lacy white socks. You didn't see that every day. Most kids wore sneakers to recess. And most kids didn't stand erect, nose raised ever so slightly. But that was how Noreen stood as she

1

peered down over the pitcher's shoulder. You'd have thought she was a queen inspecting her troops.

Calliope smirked. Noreen, the teacher's pet who raised her hand to answer any question, who never lost her homework and finished every assignment on time—that was the girl Calliope knew from school. Such a girl was a stickler about the rules but she had to be a wimp on the playground. Calliope watched closely as Thomas swaggered to home plate.

Tall and broad, Thomas was built like the rear wall of the school. He could kick the ball out of the playground. If he connected, that is. Thomas had a hard time raising his giant foot in time to kick the ball.

Hunched forward, eyes focused on the big red ball in the pitcher's hands, Thomas looked determined today. And no wonder. It was the bottom of the ninth inning, one out gone and the game tied 3 to 3. If he kicked the ball out of the playground now, their team would win and he'd be a hero.

Swoosh! went Thomas's foot as he missed the first pitch. He missed the second pitch as well. The third pitch skittered along the lumpy ground toward the plate. Thomas's eyes darted frantically, trying to keep up with the ball. He cocked back his leg and swung it forward mightily.

Calliope rose up on her knees for a good look,

but Thomas's foot again swooshed past the ball. Or did it?

Thomas certainly didn't think so. He swore his foot had tipped the ball, which—if true—would give him another chance at the plate.

But Noreen wouldn't hear of it. No matter how hard Thomas blustered, Noreen wouldn't give in. Not even when a glowering Thomas looked ready to charge the mound like an angry bull.

Wow, thought Calliope. There was only one other girl who had stood up to Thomas, and that was her. Maybe Noreen wasn't as prissy as she looked.

Calliope stood. It was her turn at the plate. Could she succeed where Thomas had failed? She imagined herself prancing across home plate as her team cheered.

Hey, it could happen.

Oh, Come On

Calliope wasn't half as strong as Thomas but she had an eagle eye. Her foot clobbered the first pitch, sending the ball wobbling over Noreen's head and into the outfield.

Calliope dashed toward first base. She looked out to left field, where Joey tried to scoop up the spinning ball in one hand and then fumbled it. Yes! Head down, Calliope raced on.

As she rounded second and then third base, Calliope again looked out to left field. Joey held the ball in both hands above his head. He heaved the ball to home plate. *Plop, plop, plop,* the ball bounced past Calliope.

Jamie, the girl playing catcher, grabbed the ball and stepped between Calliope and home plate.

Now, most kids would have slowed down or veered away, accepting defeat. But not Calliope. She dropped bottom-first and slid into Jamie. The catcher buckled. As Jamie collapsed, Calliope felt the ball glance off the back of her neck. The touch was so slight and so fleeting that she doubted the tumbling Jamie even knew she'd tagged her.

But Noreen knew. She immediately cried, "Out!"

Calliope jumped to her feet. "Oh, come on," she said, stomping her foot on home plate. "No way am I out."

"I'm afraid you are," said Noreen, who had positioned herself between home plate and the pitcher's mound. She stood as straight as a ruler, arms crossed.

Calliope shouted over her shoulder. "Jamie, am I out?"

A dusty Jamie stood behind home plate. She stared down at the kickball, which she rolled in her hands. After a moment she looked up and answered Calliope with a shrug.

Good old Jamie. You could always count on her to keep things muddled. "See?" said Calliope, pointing at her indecisive tagger. "Jamie says I'm safe."

"It doesn't matter what Jamie says," retorted Noreen. "Mrs. Perkins named me ump and I say you're out."

True enough. But that didn't make Noreen right, did it? Not in Calliope's playbook. She glanced toward the back of the playground. There stood Mrs. Perkins, still huddled with the other teachers. Mrs. Perkins kept her students in sight, but no way could she see them well. And that meant Calliope had some wiggle room to make a little trouble.

Calliope looked back at Noreen's shiny black shoes and lacy white socks. How lovely—and easy to soil. She marched off home plate and stomped in a circle around Noreen. Dirt and stones splattered Noreen's feet.

Not once did Noreen flick her perfect ponytail in irritation. She raised her sharp nose ever so slightly and smiled down on the circling Calliope.

It was a smile that made Calliope feel three years old. She cut short her war dance.

Noreen raised each of her feet and gently shook off the dirt and stones.

Calliope couldn't help smiling. Lacy socks, my foot. Noreen acted dainty but she was about as delicate as her teenage brother Frederick's crowbar. And just as steely.

Noreen returned Calliope's smile. The way they grinned at each other, you'd have thought the two of them were the best of friends all the time. And, in fact, Calliope was having a good time. She loved a

good argument. And judging by the twinkle in her opponent's eye, Noreen did too.

Calliope, however, was no Thomas. She wouldn't glower for a minute and then stomp off in defeat. No, she was just beginning to fight.

Calliope kept smiling, if only to buy time. She plunged both hands into the pockets of her jean shorts and thought. If arguing wouldn't change Noreen's mind, then what would? The answer, she found, was in the bottom of her left pocket.

A Little Something for Your Nose

Calliope sidled up to Noreen, draping an arm over her shoulder. "Why fight?"

"We're not fighting," said Noreen, pulling away from Calliope's touch. "You're out and that's that."

Pouting, as if to say she was hurt, Calliope said, "Can't we be friends?"

Noreen grunted.

"Look," said Calliope, withdrawing the hand from her left pocket, "I have something for you."

Calliope raised her closed hand to Noreen's nose and then opened her palm. In it lay a small piece of curved plastic.

Coolly Noreen eyed Calliope's offering. That's right, Noreen. Take a good look, thought Calliope.

She'd never met a kid who could resist a nose harp, an item more sought after than even the kazoo.

After a moment Noreen uncrossed her arms and plucked the nose harp from Calliope's hand. The instrument dangled from Noreen's fingertips as if it were a dirty tissue.

"Go on," coaxed Calliope. "Try it." She slid her arm off Noreen's shoulder and stepped back.

By now kids had gathered around Calliope and Noreen in a semicircle. Even the outfielders had come in for a closer look. No one at Indian Trail Elementary had ever seen Noreen put anything up her nose. Not even a straw at lunch when the cafeteria monitor's back was turned. They weren't disappointed.

Delicately Noreen fitted the small feet of the harp into each of her nostrils. The harp's arched body curled back along the contour of her nose. Noreen stared down crossed-eyed at the harp, looking confused as to what to do next.

Geez, thought Calliope, Noreen was like a kid who had been grounded so long she'd forgotten how to play. Well, then, Calliope would just have to teach her. "You blow," offered Calliope, tapping her nose.

"Huh?" said Noreen, keeping her eyes fixed on the harp.

"Through your nose," said Calliope, snorting loudly twice.

Noreen nodded, closed her eyes and blew through her nose. The harp squeaked once like a mouse with its tail caught in a door.

The surrounding half circle of kids tittered.

"Not bad, not bad," said Calliope. "But this time blow harder."

Again Noreen closed her eyes. But this time she sucked in a chestful of air. She blew so hard her face wrinkled with effort. The harp honked like an angry goose.

The semicircle of kids erupted in applause.

Noreen opened her eyes, smiled faintly and curtsied. The harp dangled from one nostril but she didn't seem to mind. In fact, she stood so straight and tall it seemed that she was proud to have a harp dangling from her nose. She flashed Calliope a smile.

Calliope again draped an arm around Noreen's shoulder. This time Noreen didn't shrink away.

"Now how about it," Calliope cooed, "can't I be safe, just this once?"

"Safe from what?"

Calliope looked up. Mrs. Perkins had returned. She stood, hands on hips, at the edge of the group of kids huddled around Noreen. "What happened to kickball?" Mrs. Perkins asked suspiciously.

"Nothing," said Noreen, wiping the harp out of her nose. She slipped free of Calliope's embrace. "I was just telling Calliope that she was *out*."

Mrs. Perkins's eyes narrowed on Calliope. "Do we have a problem with that?"

"No, ma'am," murmured Calliope. She retreated behind home plate and plopped down cross-legged in the dirt. She tried to glare up at Noreen but she couldn't keep her mouth turned down. It kept breaking into a smile. She had to admit it. Arguing with Noreen had been fun. Did Noreen feel the same way?

Calliope glanced up at Noreen, who was watching the other kids wander off the ballfield toward the playground's swing sets. Again she stood erect, ponytail sticking straight out, eyes ahead. Calliope couldn't tell what she was thinking. And that made Calliope mad!

A Pickle for Your Thoughts

"The usual?" asked the man in the stained apron. He stood behind a weathered counter between two glass display cases.

"Yes, please, Herschel," answered Calliope. She unslung her backpack, dropped to her knees and pressed her face against the case on the left. Among the bowls of cream cheese and pickled fish stood a tall glass jar with murky green water. Herschel plunged a gloved hand into the liquid and chased a slippery green torpedo.

When Herschel nabbed the torpedo, Calliope stood. She put two quarters on the counter.

"You sure do like these kosher dills," said Herschel as he wrapped a bulky pickle in wax paper.

Calliope nodded as she received the waxy

package. Hungrily she unwrapped the paper and bit into the pickle. Its vinegary taste curled her tongue and she smiled. She sucked on the pickle as if it were a giant pacifier.

Calliope looked across at Herschel, who rubbed his lined forehead.

"Try one," mumbled Calliope, nodding toward the pickle jar.

"Might as well," sighed Herschel. He retrieved a pickle for himself. Leaning back against a rear counter, he rolled the pickle around in his mouth as if it were an unlit cigar. After a moment he sighed again.

"You can tell me," said Calliope, lowering her pickle. "What's wrong?"

"I'm getting too old for this," said Herschel.

"What do you mean?"

"I mean, business isn't so good anymore." Herschel nodded toward a rack of dusty bags of potato chips.

Calliope looked around the deli too. For the first time she noticed that she was the only one in the store. "I'll tell you what," she said. "From now on I'll come every day after school and twice on Saturday."

"I hope not!" said Herschel. "You only come when

you're blue." He studied Calliope for a moment. "Now tell me. What's bothering you today?"

Calliope's head drooped. "Herschel," she said, staring at her feet, "I've finally met my match."

"I don't believe you," said Herschel.

"I'm afraid it's true," sighed Calliope. "I've been bested by a girl in lacy white socks."

Herschel chuckled.

"It's not funny."

"Well, you don't sound angry."

"I know," said Calliope, mystified. "But I should be angry, shouldn't I?"

Herschel shrugged. "My wife drives me crazy, but we've been happily married for forty years."

Now it was Calliope's turn to laugh.

Herschel wagged his pickle at Calliope. "Tell me about this girl. Does she live around here?"

"I don't think so," said Calliope. "At least I've never seen her."

"Maybe I have. What does she look like?"

How to describe Noreen? Calliope slurped on her juicy pickle, lost in thought. In the middle of an especially long vinegary slurp, it came to her. Why not *show* Herschel who Noreen was?

Calliope lovingly laid her pickle on the deli counter. Then she grabbed her thick blond hair in one hand and pulled it back in a tight ponytail. Next she stood erect, head held high. Nose raised ever so slightly, she looked squarely at Herschel. "This," she said, "is Noreen."

"Wow," said Herschel. "She looks like quite a gal."

"Oh, she is, she is," said Calliope, letting down her hair.

"You sound surprised," said Herschel.

"Well, I just never expected to like her. We're so different."

"Ha, now I see," said Herschel.

Calliope looked confused.

"Here," said Herschel, laying his pickle next to Calliope's, "allow me to demonstrate." He clenched each hand into a fist and raised them level, inches apart, in front of Calliope. "Pretend each of my fists is a magnet."

"What?" said Calliope with a laugh.

"Come on now," said Herschel. "I know you're good at pretending."

"Okay," said Calliope, concentrating on the fists in front of her.

"Now, what happens when the positive end of one magnet faces the negative end of another?"

Calliope knew the answer to that. She had a shoe-box full of magnets at home. "They're pulled together, of course."

"Exactly," said Herschel, slapping his fists together. "Opposites attract."

"So," said Calliope, still pondering Herschel's connected fists, "I like Noreen because she is so different from me?"

Herschel lowered his fists. "I knew you were a smart girl."

"But why, Herschel? Why would opposites attract?"

"Good question," said Herschel, and picked up his pickle between his middle and index finger. He put the pickle back in his mouth and puffed on it like a cigar, looking thoughtfully up at the ceiling. "I guess you'll just have to figure that out."

Calliope picked up her pickle too and sucked on it again. She sucked so hard on her pickle that it squeaked for mercy.

The Lofty Hideout

It was warm for October, the kind of day you didn't want to waste. The kind of day that called for something, well, daring. So Calliope made a bet with herself. If she didn't see someone she knew in the next five seconds, she'd hop to the park on one leg, pickle in mouth.

As she stood outside Herschel's Deli, her eyes swept the row of storefronts that lined the street while her brain ticked off the seconds. One, two, three, four. "Hello, Mrs. Johnson," Calliope blurted out.

A white-haired woman, standing broom in hand outside a storefront, turned and smiled. "Why, hello, Calliope."

"You don't know how glad I am to see you, Mrs. Johnson."

"Is something wrong, dear?"

"Not anymore." And with that, Calliope strode off down the street.

Ahead of Calliope loomed a neighborhood of great houses. Tall and uneven, with big wooden porches and sprawling back additions, these houses made her think of sleeping dinosaurs.

Atop the high steps of a yellow wooden house sat a boy fumbling with the knotty laces of some Rollerblades.

"Hi, Tommy," said Calliope as she passed.

"Hey," answered Tommy, bent over his skates in concentration.

The big houses ended at a small park shaped like a wedge of pizza. Black dirt pizza with a grassy topping, thought Calliope as she entered the park.

At the tip of the park Calliope came to a row of rusty swings, each one creaking with the pumping effort of a little pair of legs. Some of the kids waved at her. She smiled and turned to look behind her. There stood a tall tree with a wide trunk. Many a boy in the neighborhood had tried and failed to climb this tree.

The problem, Calliope had figured out a while ago, was that boys tried to muscle their way up. A tree like this required smarts.

Calliope glanced back to the swinging kids to

make sure no one was looking at her. Then she tossed the remaining stub of pickle into the bushes and crouched like a runner at the start of a race. Head down, she counted to herself. "One, two." At "three" she bolted toward the tree. Her racing feet carried her high up the trunk.

She kept her eyes focused on the tree's first limb, jutting out about five feet up. When her Keds began to slip, she thrust out both arms. Her fingers grabbed the limb. There was just enough momentum left from her running start to carry her, guided by her grip, atop the branch. From there on up it was an easy climb, with plenty of thick branches clumped together. Calliope climbed up and up until she reached a broad limb with a spot worn in the shape of her bottom.

This was Calliope's hideout, a place where she could spy on the world without the world spying back. She straddled the worn branch, legs swinging. Leaning against the tree, she sighed.

It was time to visit Dad.

Opposites Do Attract

From her lofty perch Calliope scanned the rolling terrain carpeted with houses and big trees. About a half mile away a clearing rose like an exposed shoulder. Tombstones dotted the clearing. Under one of them lay Dad. Which one, Calliope didn't know, didn't care to know. She knew he was there somewhere and that was good enough. She always declined Mom's frequent invitations to visit Dad's grave, because she preferred visiting like this—far enough away that it didn't seem quite so real.

Calliope closed her eyes. She saw her dad chasing her on all fours, barking like a dog. That memory faded into another. This time she saw her dad giving her her first nose harp. Her nose wriggled as she remembered the first time she'd poked the harp's plastic feet up her nostrils.

Calliope's nose held a lot of memories of Dad. She breathed deeply. Aaah. She could still smell the raw onions Dad loved to eat every morning. He said they made him feel alive. It was a feeling he liked to share with his only daughter. After eating his morning onion, he would creep into her room and breathe in her face. How many kids had a dad with oniony breath for an alarm clock?

Sometimes Calliope imagined—just for fun, mind you—that Dad was with her still. Not alive but, say, like the mist from a spray bottle. She pictured him drifting just ahead of her right shoulder. Yes, if Calliope squeezed her eyes closed really tight, her cheek could almost feel Dad's wetness. In her mind, she made Dad float ahead, a misty lookout for his only daughter. He'd snatch the last ice cream sandwich from the freezer in the school cafeteria for her. Or he'd scout out a new best friend for her. Emily—her old best friend—had moved away last year.

Calliope pictured Dad hovering above, nodding approvingly, as she conjured up Noreen for his inspection. Again Noreen stood, nose raised high, arms crossed, unflinching as Calliope kicked up a dust storm around her.

Well, Dad, what do you think? Dad didn't answer. His misty image receded into Calliope's imagination.

No matter. Calliope had an answer to her own question and this is what she thought: Herschel was right. While opposite in almost every way, she and Noreen were drawn to each other. Noreen had enjoyed arguing about kickball more than playing it, just like Calliope. The two of them could be the best of friends. Calliope was sure of it. Noreen just needed someone who could help her loosen up, laugh a little. Of course Noreen would probably never admit that. How could Calliope help Noreen see it?

Of course, thought Calliope, suddenly sitting upright. Mrs. B. She'd know what to do.

Cheerios and Orange Juice

Why was going up the tree always easier than coming down? Calliope wondered as she dangled by her weakening arms. Slowly her fingers peeled off the branch and she dropped five feet to the ground. She landed on her hands and knees in a puff of dirt. So much for a graceful descent.

Her knees stung but not as much as her pride. The kids on the swings laughed and cheered her as they would a clown rather than a hero who did what even older boys couldn't do.

Calliope tried to ignore the cheering and stood as if she'd descended like a feather carried on a breeze. This, however, turned the cheering into outright laughter.

Disgusted, Calliope wiped her knees clean and huffed off toward home.

She left the park and entered a neighborhood of small, boxy houses that lined the streets shoulder to shoulder. They looked largely identical, painted white and with little green patches of lawn.

There was one house that dared not to be white. It was purple with turquoise shutters.

This house made you want to stop and wonder. Who lived in such a place? Calliope did stop but she didn't wonder. She knew who lived inside. It was her house, where she lived with her mother and two older brothers, Jonah and Frederick.

Right now nobody was home. Mom was still at work. Jonah was in class up the street at Seton Hall University. As for her teenage brother, Frederick, he still had two hours left in high school. And after dismissal he often hung out with his friends or worked the soda fountain at Grunting's.

Calliope wasn't allowed inside her house until someone else was home. So she walked to the house next door. It was the biggest house on the street, the only one with a glassed-in vestibule.

From a side pocket in her backpack she took a key and opened the door of the large house. She stepped onto a floor of shiny little wooden tiles that squeaked under her feet as she walked down the hallway. She gave her feet a slight twist at every step.

At the end of the hallway there was a small kitchen with an old wooden table. On the table sat three cereal bowls. At one bowl squatted Mortimer, a big furry rabbit. He was white except for a black patch around one eye.

In front of the next bowl sat Mrs. Blatherhorn, a thin, gray-haired lady with a sharp nose. Calliope liked to call her Mrs. B. She sat straight-backed on the edge of her chair, her high-heeled shoes flat on the floor. Her hands rested atop a dark wooden cane. Its handle was carved into the shape of a growling, windswept head with deep eyes.

Mrs. B. turned the growling head to inspect Calliope as she entered the kitchen. "There you are," said Mrs. B. "We were about to begin without you."

Calliope plopped down in front of the third bowl. As she peered inside, the pickle in her stomach rolled over and gurgled.

"Wow," she said flatly. "Orange juice and Cheerios."

"I thought it was your favorite," said Mrs. B.

"It is, it is," said Calliope. And it was, just not after a big pickle. Nonetheless, she scooped up a heaping spoonful of Cheerios and smiled up at Mrs. B. She

raised the spoon toward her open mouth but stopped in midair.

The pickle in her stomach belched in protest. "Sorry," she mumbled.

Mrs. B. wrinkled her nose and turned to face the rabbit. "Do you smell what I smell, Mortimer?"

Mortimer twitched his nose.

"Exactly," said Mrs. B. "Pickles."

Calliope lowered her spoon. There was no fooling Mrs. B. No wonder Calliope had once thought she was a witch. Getting to know her next-door neighbor hadn't been easy. But now they were good friends. Mrs. B. even watched Calliope every day until her mom came home from work. They had a snack together every afternoon.

Calliope the Charmer

Mrs. B.'s brow wrinkled with disapproval.

"What's wrong with pickles?" Calliope challenged her.

"Nothing, I suppose," said Mrs. B. "Except they're not very ladylike."

"That's okay. I'm not a lady. I'm a kid."

Mrs. B. sighed.

Calliope smiled. How Mrs. B. loved to fuss over her and how Calliope loved to give Mrs. B. something to fuss about. It wasn't hard. Mrs. B. was very picky.

"I hope that pickle wasn't the only thing you had for lunch," said Mrs. B.

"Oh, no. That wasn't lunch."

"Good."

"I had an ice cream sandwich for lunch."

Mrs. B. frowned. "What happened to the sandwich your mother made you?"

"Ah . . . I accidentally dropped it in the trash?"

Mrs. B. arched an eyebrow.

"I mean, I threw it out."

"Calliope."

"Well, it was baloney and mayonnaise and you know how I hate that."

"Still, you don't throw away perfectly good food."

As usual, Mrs. B. was right. "Sorry."

Mrs. B. accepted the apology with a nod and then began her daily grilling. Had Calliope remembered to turn in her homework? What day were class conferences? How had she done on her math test?

Tat ta tat tat, tat ta tat tat. Calliope listened to the driving beat of Mrs. B's questions, which sounded like her college brother typing on his old manual typewriter. How different Mrs. B. sounded from Mom. Calliope pictured her mother talking. It was more like the crash of cymbals.

"What? The school play is tomorrow? Why didn't you tell me?"

"I did, Mom. I did," Calliope would answer.

It was hard to get through to her mom. She was always on the move—picking up laundry, talking on the phone, cooking dinner, rushing out the door to work or doing a million chores. Calliope broke into a cold sweat just thinking about all her mother did to keep the family together.

Of course her two brothers could help out some, but it was easier to drag a sack of stones than to get them to do anything useful. When he was home, Jonah sprawled across chairs or the sofa, reading. Ask Frederick for help and he just growled.

That left Calliope, who did her best to help her mom. And the way she helped best was by taking care of herself. And nobody had to nag her to brush her teeth or fold the laundry.

Calliope was proud of her independence. Yet there were times when she would actually try to forget brushing her teeth to see if Mom would notice.

In her rush Mom wouldn't always pick up on Calliope's smelly breath, but Mrs. B. had never missed yet. Calliope found that comforting.

"Calliope?"

"Ah, sorry," said Calliope, looking up into Mrs. B's reddening face.

"The math test?" Mrs. B. asked again.

Ah yes, the math test. Calliope had done all right but not well enough to satisfy Mrs. B. So she distracted Mrs. B. with a question of her own. "Did you ever like someone more than she liked you?"

Mrs. B. stopped midquestion and silently considered Calliope.

"I mean," continued Calliope, "how do you make someone really like you?"

Mrs. B. grinned.

"I'm serious," protested Calliope.

"I'm sorry, dear, I know you are. It's just that, of all people, you should know the answer to that question."

"I should?"

"Remember? I wanted to drive you out of the neighborhood. Now look at us."

"Yeah," Calliope said dreamily. She and Mrs. B. simultaneously reached to scratch Mortimer behind the ears.

Nose down in his bowl, Mortimer bubbled the orange juice as he was scratched.

"How'd I do it?" Calliope wondered aloud.

"Do what?"

"Win you over."

"You charmed the pants off of me," said Mrs. B. as if she still couldn't believe it.

"I did, didn't I?" Calliope's lips curved into a smile. Of course! That was it. She'd charm Noreen right out of her lacy socks.

The Bobbing Head

Mom liked to say that Calliope had a smile that could melt an Eskimo Pie. Its warmth came not so much from Calliope's less-than-straight teeth but from her eyes. They twinkled with "devilish intent." At least that was what Mrs. B. said.

Calliope turned now to give Noreen one of her most devilish smiles. The two sat side by side in class, but today Noreen gazed ahead as if the chair next to her were empty.

Noreen sat erect, feet flat on the floor and ponytail standing out at attention.

Maybe Noreen was still sore about the kickball game, or maybe she was just being difficult. Either way, Calliope wasn't giving up. She stretched her smile until it hurt.

Still Noreen looked ahead, eyes tracking the approach of Mrs. Perkins. Their teacher held a stack of math work sheets and handed them out as she walked among the desks.

"Thank you, Mrs. Perkins," said Noreen as she took a work sheet.

"You're most welcome," replied a smiling Mrs. Perkins.

That was Noreen for you. She always knew how to make grown-ups smile. It was as if she were one herself, only shrunken down to kid size.

Holding out a work sheet, Mrs. Perkins smiled expectantly at Calliope.

Sorry, Mrs. Perkins, but Calliope was not Noreen. No way was she going to thank her teacher for a math work sheet. Calliope's smile vanished and she took the work sheet with a nod of resignation.

Mrs. Perkins sighed as if disappointed and moved on.

Calliope studied the long rows of addition problems and wondered. How could she persuade Noreen that together they added up to something bigger than each of them alone?

Lost in thought, Calliope put down the work sheet and slipped both hands into the pockets of her jean shorts. As usual they were stuffed with the bizarre and the amusing.

There was, of course, the nose harp. Her exploring hands fingered a thick rubber band, a toy soldier and a small folding magnifying glass. She released each of these things and moved on.

Then the fingers of her left hand curled around something small, round and hairy. Calliope smiled. Now, here was something with real possibilities. Carefully she snuck her hand out of the pocket and into the hollow of her desk.

Had Mrs. Perkins noticed? She stood up front. Like a searchlight, her eyes swept the rows of number-crunching kids.

With her free hand Calliope picked up a pencil and hunched over her desk. She looked like a model student.

Mrs. Perkins's sweeping eyes stopped on Calliope for a moment and then moved on.

Calliope slowly withdrew her hand from the desk and glanced down. There in the palm of her hand lay a Barbie head with a blond ponytail.

Barbie heads, Calliope had learned, were powerful things. Flash one in the supermarket and even adults couldn't help smiling. In the hands of a master such as herself they could make the most serious of kids bubble with laughter.

But how could Calliope use the head now? The answer came from above.

"Mrs. Perkins?" crackled a speaker in a corner of the ceiling.

Mrs. Perkins looked up. "Yes?"

"We need you in the office for a moment."

"I'll be right there," she said. "Jamie."

"Yes, ma'am," said Jamie from the back of the class.

"Come," said Mrs. Perkins, "it's your turn to be in charge."

"Are you sure?"

Mrs. Perkins nodded, patting the high seat of her stool.

Jamie rose hesitantly and shuffled to the front of the class. As she sat down on the stool, Mrs. Perkins grasped her shoulder. "I know," Mrs. Perkins announced, "that everyone is going to be very well behaved for Jamie while I'm gone."

With that, Mrs. Perkins departed, leaving Jamie hunched atop the stool studying her cuticles.

Oh, thank you, thank you, Mrs. Perkins, thought Calliope. She slipped the Barbie head onto the tip of a pinky and turned to smile at the girl sitting next to her.

Noreen, prepare to laugh.

Calliope leaned forward, raising the Barbie head just above the lip of Noreen's desk. Then she began bobbing the Barbie head along the desk's edge.

Noreen, head pointed down at her work sheet, glanced sideways at the bobbing plastic head.

"Yoo-hoo," squeaked Calliope, nodding the head at Noreen, "I'm spying on you."

For a second Noreen's cheek dimpled. Then she pulled her eyes back to the work sheet.

"Yoo-hoo," Calliope squeaked more loudly.

Noreen turned her face away as if to pretend there was no plastic head bobbing along the edge of the desk.

Calliope had never seen someone work so hard not to laugh. "I said," she nearly shouted, "yoo-hoo."

Noreen bit her lower lip and pressed her pencil down so hard the tip of it broke off.

I've got her now, thought Calliope. She bobbed the Barbie head in a victory dance. The dance, however, did not last long. It stopped when Calliope heard a familiar voice overhead.

"Surrender, Barbie."

Calliope looked up to see Mrs. Perkins. She stood with a hand outstretched, palm up. An index finger summoned the Barbie head.

With a sigh Calliope sat up. She dropped the head into Mrs. Perkins's palm.

"Thank you," said Mrs. Perkins. "I'll just add this to my collection."

That collection was in a top drawer of Mrs.

Perkins's desk. It was filled with heads, fangs, whistles and such, all of which had at one time belonged to Calliope.

Calliope remembered each and every one of those things with a mixture of loss and pride. Who else had their own drawer in the teacher's desk? Yet that drawer was getting awfully full with so much of Calliope's stuff.

In irritation, Calliope twitched her nose, not unlike Mortimer. From the seat next to her she heard a soft giggling. She turned to see Noreen, face reddened, a hand covering her mouth.

"What's so funny?" said Calliope irritably.

Noreen pointed to Calliope's nose.

Again Calliope's nose twitched in irritation and Noreen giggled.

"Noreen," said Mrs. Perkins.

"Sorry," said Noreen, trying to control herself.

But Calliope made sure it was no use. She began to furiously twitch her nose.

Noreen's giggling rose out of her like bubbles in a soft drink. Calliope began giggling too.

Noreen laughed at Calliope's laughing at her. The girls collapsed into each other's arms, eyes wet with laughter.

"Does this mean we're good friends now?" Calliope whispered into Noreen's ear.

Noreen nodded.

"Pinky shake on it?" said Calliope, pulling back and extending her pinky.

Noreen firmly hooked Calliope's pinky with her own and shook it hard.

What Am I, a Tea Biscuit?

Calliope liked to think of her imagination as a rubber band. Every day she tried to stretch it into a new and wonderful shape.

Most kids, Calliope believed, had their own rubber band. Except Noreen seemed to have left hers crumpled and dusty in a forgotten corner of her brain.

That was a problem Calliope took it upon herself to fix. She would help Noreen rediscover her imagination. She would help her learn how to use it too. After all, what were friends for?

Calliope sat now with Noreen at a low table in the school cafeteria. Around them buzzed hundreds of munching, drumming and chortling kids.

"Aren't they beautiful?" sighed Calliope, looking

down into an opened hand. In her palm lay a pair of pink plastic fangs. Calliope held them out for Noreen to admire.

Noreen peered into Calliope's hand and grimaced.

Calliope lowered her hand. "Noreen."

"What?"

"You *do* want to be my friend, right?"

Noreen didn't answer.

"Well?"

"Yes," snapped Noreen. "But what's that got to do with a pair of cheap plastic fangs?"

Calliope shook her head. Noreen had so much to learn. "Don't think of them as cheap and plastic. Think of them as magical, something that can turn you into a vampire."

"Yeah, right," scoffed Noreen.

Calliope pressed the fangs into Noreen's hand. "Just try them and you'll see what I'm talking about."

"No way," said Noreen, pressing the fangs back into Calliope's hand.

"I don't get it," said Calliope. "You stuck that nose harp up your nose."

"That was different."

"How?"

"Call me strange, but I don't like putting weird plastic stuff in my mouth."

"Well, sorry, but you have to," said Calliope. "How else am I going to teach you how to make believe?"

"Easy," said Noreen. "We'll *pretend* I already know how to make believe."

"Very funny," said Calliope, pressing the fangs back into Noreen's hand. "But you forget that I have a reputation to keep up. What will everyone say if they find out my newest friend can't even pretend she's a vampire? I mean, that's Make-believe 101."

Noreen raised her nose and sniffed.

"Come on," said Calliope. "It will be fun."

"Well . . ."

"Look, didn't I make you laugh in class yesterday?"

"Yes," said Noreen, smiling.

"Well, this is going to be even more fun," said Calliope, pressing the fangs back into Noreen's hand. "I promise."

Noreen glared at the fangs.

"Go on," coaxed Calliope, "try them. I promise they won't bite."

With a sigh Noreen picked up the fangs and slid them into her mouth. "Yuck," she mumbled. "They taste awful."

"You'll get used to it," said Calliope. She tilted her head and leaned toward Noreen.

"Now," said Calliope, pointing to her exposed neck, "take a bite."

Noreen stood and bent forward, pressing her fangs against Calliope's neck.

Calliope felt a ticklish scratching under her ear and frowned.

"What am I, a tea biscuit?" she scolded Noreen.

"No," mumbled Noreen, her mouth still pressed against Calliope's neck.

"Then don't nibble me—bite!" Calliope chomped her teeth together loudly to make the point.

Startled, Noreen stumbled backward into her chair.

Calliope couldn't help smiling. It wasn't often you caught Noreen with even a hair out of place. Now she looked as if she'd been through a wind tunnel, her forehead covered with wisps of hair.

Noreen frowned at Calliope's smile. She pulled her hair back tight into a ponytail and straightened her fangs. Her eyes narrowed to slits. A low hiss came from deep inside her chest and she curled her upper lip.

"That's it, that's it," Calliope said excitedly. Again she offered her neck to Noreen.

Noreen studied Calliope for a moment and then sprang. Her fangs clamped on Calliope's neck.

Calliope's eyes watered but she didn't cry. "Very nice," she said through clenched teeth. "I think you've got the hang of it now."

Noreen shook Calliope's neck like a dog with a good bone.

"You can let go now."

Noreen growled.

"I said . . . *let go*." Calliope raised her feet and pressed them hard against Noreen's stomach.

Pop! Noreen flew off, landing bottom-first back in her seat. There she sprawled, fangs dangling half out of her mouth. Her white blouse sported a faint pair of pigeon-toed footprints.

Uh-oh, thought Calliope, remembering how particular Noreen was about her clothes. But Noreen either didn't see the footprints or didn't mind them. She gazed off into space dreamily.

Well, I'll be, thought Calliope. She'd done it, she'd taught Noreen how to make believe. Arms folded, Calliope admired her handiwork. This must have been how Dad felt when he taught her how to ride a bicycle without training wheels.

Noreen stirred as if awakening. Her dreamy look changed into one of someone caught with her hand in a cookie jar. She spit out the fangs, sat up straight and retightened her ponytail.

"Very interesting," she said, returning Calliope's fangs.

"Interesting?" said Calliope with a chuckle.

"Yes. Definitely."

Calliope shook her head.

"But," said Noreen pointedly, "not quite as interesting as what I have."

Here we go again, thought Calliope. Noreen sure liked to challenge her. Maybe that was why Calliope liked Noreen so much. Again Calliope saw Herschel's fists, except this time one looked like her face and the other like Noreen's. Herschel smacked the fists together with a loud whap.

"Oh, yes," Noreen piped up, trying to keep Calliope's attention.

"What are you talking about?" said Calliope, shaking off the image of the smacking fists.

"Oh, nothing. Just a little something my father brought me."

"What? A new dust ruffle for your bed?" scoffed Calliope.

Noreen just smiled.

"All right, then," said Calliope. "Let's see it."

"Oh, it's not here."

Calliope smirked as if she'd called Noreen's bluff.

But Noreen looked anything but defeated. Confidently she added, "It's at home. Would you like to come over and see it?"

Now, no one Calliope knew had ever been invited over to Noreen's house. So, naturally, Calliope grew excited. This must mean they were indeed friends.

"You bet!" Calliope caught herself. She shouldn't sound too eager. That would be unbecoming, as Noreen would say. "Why, yes," said Calliope, imitating Noreen. "That would be lovely."

"Say, then, tomorrow after school?"

A Family Portrait

Calliope sat cross-legged behind several mounds of wrinkled clothes. Across the room, her mom sat at a small desk. She paid bills while talking on a portable phone wedged between her shoulder and ear. Mom looked up for a moment, mouthing the words "get cracking."

Okay, thought Calliope—get cracking—and she cracked her bubble gum in what she thought was a very clever response.

Mom didn't laugh. She stared at her daughter blankly for a moment before talking into the phone and writing more checks.

That's Mom for you, thought Calliope. Too busy to get a stupid little joke. There was a lot Mom didn't see. Smiling, Calliope patted a pile of under-wear at her side.

The pile quivered; then out from under it popped a furry whiskered nose. It wriggled, which meant "thank you" in rabbit-ese.

You didn't have to be fluent in rabbit-ese, as Calliope had become, to understand Mortimer's gratitude. He was cage-free and in the living room. Of course, he wasn't supposed to be in the living room, especially at night when Mom was home.

But hey, if Mom was too busy to notice, what was the difference?

With one eye on Mom, Calliope raised the top of the underwear pile to check on Mortimer. Dangling from his mouth was a pair of Frederick's favorite boxer shorts, which were imprinted with little cheeseburgers.

"Mortimer," scolded Calliope, yanking the under-wear away.

Calliope had spoken too sharply. Mom looked up from her bills. "What?" said Mom, looking at Calliope.

"Ah . . . my, look at the time," said Calliope to her mother. She dropped the top of the underwear pile back on Mortimer's head.

"You're right," said Mom, looking at her wrist-watch. Briskly she resumed writing checks and talk-ing on the phone.

Calliope examined the boxers in her hand. Mortimer had gnawed away a little cheeseburger, leaving a hole the size of a dime. Fingering the hole, Calliope had a fun idea.

She raised the boxers to her face and pressed the hole against one eye. Now she was a famous photographer on a dangerous assignment: to capture the elusive Day family on film in their natural habitat.

Aha, thought Calliope, scanning the room, there's one of them now. It was Frederick in his favorite chair. Frederick sat, head and feet slopped over the arms of the chair, like a big fish in a small basket.

Both hands rested on a bulging stomach that rose as he sighed and stared off into the corner. Calliope bet he was thinking about his next meal, although they'd all just had dinner.

"Smile," Calliope called to him, peering through the hole in the underwear.

Frederick's head turned slowly toward her.

"*Click!*" Calliope said loudly.

Frederick's glazed eyes brightened, focused on Calliope for a moment, then dulled again. He returned to staring at the corner.

How do you like that? Frederick found a dusty corner more interesting than his little sister.

Calliope turned her gaze sharply from Frederick and continued scanning the room. It wasn't long

before she spotted Jonah, who lay faceup on the couch. Head resting against the arm, he was reading a big book balanced on his stomach.

Jonah was always reading big books. It was part of his studies at Seton Hall University.

Seton Hall was just up the street and Jonah lived at home. Probably so he didn't have to fold his own laundry.

"Smile," Calliope called through the underwear.

Jonah's head turned but not to face Calliope. It fell sideways into the pages of the book. She heard a loud snore.

He was sleeping. Sleeping while his little sister sat here folding his stinky old underwear. The nerve, thought Calliope as she threw down her underwear camera. Such behavior could not go unpunished.

Calliope rested her head in a cupped hand. What would Dad, that master joker, have done? At the thought of her father, Calliope's nose stung with the smell of raw onions.

Bubble Gum Shorts

Calliope remembered her dad standing amid the dirty clothes littering the floor of Jonah's room. "From now on," Dad had declared, "I will wear on my head any clothes you don't put in the laundry."

Jonah, a pimply teenager at the time, just snorted. He didn't take Dad seriously until the evening he brought home his first girlfriend. Dad introduced himself to the girl while wearing a pair of Jonah's underwear on his head. From that day you couldn't find so much as a dirty sock on the floor of Jonah's room.

Dad had been so clever. He was serious in a silly way. Just look at how he'd come up with Calliope's name. Dad had named her after Calliope, the Greek Muse of great poetry. The Muses were nine ancient spirits whose job it was to inspire humans to greatness. Calliope, of course, was the oldest and boss of her eight sister Muses.

Her name was a tough one to live up to, but Calliope did the best she could. And now, even though he was gone, Dad helped. Calliope's memory of him gave her an idea about how to win Jonah's respect.

Mom looked up from her check-writing, this time to see Calliope neatly folding a pair of Jonah's white briefs. If only Mom had looked a moment earlier. She would have caught Calliope putting her bubble gum in the bottom of Jonah's undies.

Never again would Jonah forget who folded his underwear.

Calliope read her mom's approval as a sign that now would be a good time to ask about going to Noreen's after school. "Mom?"

"Yes, my butterfly?" Mom put down her pen and telephone and looked intently at her daughter.

"Mom," said Calliope, blushing. She glanced at Frederick. Good, he was still staring at the wall. Mom's use of Calliope's baby nickname had gone unnoticed. "I told you not to call me that anymore," Calliope whispered harshly.

Mom smiled wickedly. "How did our little song go?"

"Don't start," warned Calliope.

Mom ignored her daughter's warning. She began humming and singing. " 'So bright, so beautiful, my little butterfly—' "

" 'Soar, high, high and away,' " Calliope interrupted.

"That's not how it goes," said Mom, frowning.

It was Calliope's turn to smile wickedly.

Mom crossed her arms. "Come on," she said. "I know you remember the words."

How could Calliope forget them? Mom had sung her little song to Calliope every night for years. It was the only way Calliope would go to sleep.

Calliope no longer needed lullabies. They were for little kids. She was big now and she didn't want anyone—especially her brothers—to think otherwise.

Calliope crossed her arms the way her mom did and looked her in the eye.

"Well?" said Mom, staring back.

The two of them often ended up like this, eye to eye, neither wanting to give ground. Why couldn't Mom be more like Dad? He always got Calliope to do what he wanted but he made it seem like her idea.

While staring back defiantly, Calliope knew she would have to sing at least a line or two of the butterfly song. Otherwise Mom would get grumpy. And a grumpy mom wasn't likely to let Calliope go to Noreen's after school.

Calliope lowered her gaze and mumbled, " 'So bright, so beautiful, my little butterfly.' "

Smiling, Mom cupped a hand to her ear. "I can't hear you."

Calliope looked up and boomed, " 'Let me hold you in my hand. Keep you safe and warm. Wouldn't that be grand?' "

There was a loud creak and Calliope turned to see Frederick sitting up and smirking at her.

Oh, brother, she thought, here it comes.

She's Not a Twerp

"**C**ome here, my little butterfly," said Frederick, beckoning with his forefinger. "Let me pin you to my wall."

Calliope heaved Frederick's gnawed underwear at him.

Mom rose to leave and Calliope blurted, "Mom, can I go to Noreen's after school tomorrow?"

At first Mom didn't answer. She sat back down and studied Calliope for a moment. "Do I know this Noreen?"

"Remember? The school play. She wore the most perfect, beautiful costume."

Mom's eyes scanned Calliope's forehead as if searching her daughter's memory for a picture of Noreen.

Calliope obliged, remembering Noreen in sequined robes and a crown.

"Oh, yes," said Mom, smiling. "Now I remember. Noreen was the queen in the school play."

"That twerp?" snorted Frederick.

"She's not a twerp," said Calliope.

"She looked like a lovely girl to me," said Mom.

"See?" said Calliope, sticking her tongue out at Frederick.

"Where does Noreen live?" asked Mom.

"Newstead," said Calliope, repeating what Noreen had told her. Calliope had never been to Newstead, a neighborhood atop a big hill overlooking the town. She had been to a nearby park, where her family used to go on a clear Sunday to admire the skyline of New York. The tall buildings shimmered again in her imagination, and she really wanted to go see what the rest of Newstead looked like.

"Too far," said Frederick with finality.

Calliope turned to glare at her brother. That was just like him, trying to ruin everything. Were all teenage brothers as maddening as Frederick? One minute he wanted to pin her to his wall. The next you'd think he was her dad.

Take a recent family outing to McDonald's. After dinner Calliope had climbed atop the restaurant's big plastic slide. Frederick had called her a big baby for playing on the little kiddy rides. But when some kid shoved her off the top of the slide, Frederick had rushed in to catch her. Once she was snug in Frederick's brawny arms, she was pretty sure he gave her an extra squeeze—suspiciously close to a hug! Maybe Frederick really did love her. He just didn't want anyone—especially Calliope—to know it.

"I'm afraid Frederick's right," said Mom. "Newstead is on the other side of town. How would I get you there after school?"

"You don't have to," Calliope said, shooting Frederick a look of triumph. "I can ride Noreen's bus home with her."

"What if she gets on the wrong bus?" countered Frederick. "She's only nine, after all."

"Hah, that shows how little you know," huffed Calliope. "I'm nine and a half and I won't get on the wrong bus."

"Ah, but is transportation the real question here?" It was Jonah. He spoke, eyes closed, lying faceup on the couch. Wagging a finger at the ceiling, he continued, "I think not."

"What do you mean?" said Mom, sounding concerned. She set great store by what Jonah said.

"I mean," said Jonah, lecturing the ceiling, "what

if Calliope does find the right bus, makes it to Noreen's and returns home safely?"

Mom looked lost.

"And your point is?" put in Frederick.

"My point is this: If Calliope successfully pulls off going to her friend's, then she will have grown up a little bit more, hastening the day when she will no longer be our baby sister. Do we really want that?"

Jonah reached out and rubbed Calliope's head as if she were a puppy. She turned sharply and tried to bite his hand.

"Calliope," scolded Mom.

"Sorry," said Calliope, but she wasn't. She turned back to face Mom and didn't like what she saw. Mom studied Calliope with a sad smile.

Ooh, that Jonah! He had such a way with words. Still, she wasn't conceding defeat. She rose to her knees, hands clasped in front of her. "Please, oh, please, can I go to Noreen's?" she begged her mother.

"Well," stalled Mom. Her eyes darted between Frederick and Jonah. "If you really, really want to go . . ."

Calliope beamed. "I really, really, really want to go."

Mom nodded but she was no longer paying

attention to Calliope. Her eyes followed a pair of Frederick's underwear slinking across the floor as if it were alive.

Mortimer.

Oops . . . "Now how did that silly rabbit get in here?" said Calliope.

"I wonder . . . ," said Mom with a knowing smile.

The Red Mercedes

The bell rang, marking the end of the school day. It was time for Mrs. Perkins to divide the class for dismissal. First came the walkers, even though some in this group rode bicycles. This was Calliope's group and she was proud to be a member. They got to leave for home before anyone else.

Today Calliope didn't stand as the walkers were called. She watched them leave and wondered who came next in the pecking order of dismissal. It was a mystery to her because she usually left before the next group was called.

"Bus riders, please stand," called Mrs. Perkins. "Form a single line at the door."

Most of the kids stood and Calliope stood with

them. She moved to join the other bus riders and then stopped, noticing that Noreen was still seated.

"Where do you think you're going?" Noreen asked Calliope.

"Home with you."

"Then you'd better sit down," said Noreen.

Calliope stood, frozen in confusion.

"Calliope?" said Mrs. Perkins.

Calliope sat back down. "You don't ride the bus?" she whispered to Noreen.

Noreen shook her head slightly.

Calliope watched the bus riders file out of the room. Their departure left behind only a handful of kids.

"Okay, car riders," said Mrs. Perkins, "you may go."

"Your mom's picking you up because I'm visiting?" said Calliope excitedly.

"Of course not, silly," said Noreen.

Now Calliope was really confused.

Noreen stood and Calliope followed her to the car pool line in front of the school.

"Then who is picking you up?" said Calliope as they stood waiting in line with about two dozen kids.

"Charles, of course."

"Charles?"

Noreen didn't answer. She stood, nose raised, looking off into the distance.

Calliope studied the line of cars. One of them must hold the mysterious Charles.

Was it the Volkswagen Beetle with the flower decals? Hardly, thought Calliope, imitating Noreen. Next came a van. Six kids climbed aboard and fought over who would get what seat.

Calliope couldn't imagine Noreen participating in such a common struggle.

The most interesting car was at the end of the line. It was a big Mercedes-Benz, painted the color of red nail polish. The hard finish of the Mercedes glistened in the brilliant October sun. Calliope squinted, trying to make out the car's driver.

As the Mercedes neared, Calliope realized that squinting was pointless. The car's windows were tinted black like sunglasses. Now, you didn't see that every day.

Could this be Noreen's car? That seemed hard to believe, given Noreen's conservative black shoes and lacy white socks. Calliope imagined that her friend would raise her nose and call the owner of the bright red Mercedes a show-off.

But when the Mercedes reached Noreen it stopped. The driver's door opened and out stepped a big man in a black suit and cap. He walked over and opened the door in front of Noreen. Bowing slightly, the driver beckoned the girls to enter.

"Thank you, Charles," said Noreen. She disappeared inside the backseat of the car.

Charles turned to face Calliope. "Miss?" he said, gesturing for her to enter the Mercedes.

Calliope froze, her feet held in place by icy fingers of doubt. She'd figured Noreen's family had more money than hers. But a chauffeur? That wasn't just more money. That was rich. Calliope had never met a real rich person.

"Are you coming or what?" It was Noreen and her voice sounded far away inside the Mercedes.

Calliope's body clenched at Noreen's challenge. Of course now she would have to get into the Mercedes. No way was she going to let Noreen see that she was the least bit nervous; although the inside of the Mercedes was nothing like any car she'd ever seen.

A Cushion of Air

Calliope's last car ride had been two days ago when Mom had picked her up after school. She'd had an appointment for a regular checkup at the doctor's.

Where am I going to sit? Calliope had wondered when she opened the door of her mom's Saturn and looked inside. Books, papers and clothes sprawled across the backseat, and groceries took up the whole front passenger seat.

Calliope had decided it would be easier to slide the groceries onto the floor and then rearrange all the stuff in the back. Besides, up front was her seat, won through hours crisscrossing town with Mom on errands. After so many trips the seat had sunk into a bowl shaped like Calliope's bottom. She wondered if anybody else had noticed the seat's shape and the thought embarrassed her.

There was nothing embarrassing about the Mercedes. Although she rode in back, Calliope sat high on a round, firm seat. It felt as if she were sitting on Santa's high chair at the mall.

Calliope stretched out her legs. Goodness, her feet couldn't touch the back of the front seat.

Yes, thought Calliope, she supposed it didn't get any better than this, riding on a cushion of air and space.

She turned to look out her window. She watched as the world she knew glided by, tinged black. The Mercedes approached the row of storefronts in Calliope's neighborhood.

What luck. Out front stood Herschel, smoking a cigarette. Calliope pounded on her window and waved to get Herschel's attention. Wouldn't he be impressed with her in this fancy car?

Herschel raised his head, looking right at Calliope. She smiled in anticipation of his brown-toothed grin. In her mind she heard him say, "What, another pickle?"

But this time Herschel didn't speak. Nor did he smile. He sneered as Calliope drove past him.

"Herschel, it's me," Calliope said, pounding on

the window. Of course, she told herself, the black windows. Herschel could see only the Mercedes, which he didn't seem to like.

Calliope slumped back in her seat.

"Who are you talking to?" asked Noreen.

"Nobody," mumbled Calliope. It was funny how you could feel so small inside such a big car. She started to miss her cramped seat in Mom's Saturn.

Noreen reached over and patted Calliope's leg. "I know," she said, nodding toward the Mercedes's plush interior, "it's a little much."

Calliope didn't answer.

"I promise we're going to have fun," continued Noreen. "You're going to love the surprise I have to show you. But first you've got to relax."

"I'm relaxed," huffed Calliope, crossing her arms.

Noreen leaned back, giving Calliope a long look. Tapping her cheek, Noreen studied Calliope as if she were a picture frame she was trying to hang straight on the wall. "I know," Noreen said, "why don't you take off your shoes?"

"Really, I can?"

"Sure."

Calliope popped off her red Keds and sat cross-legged the way she would in Mom's car. Already she felt a little better.

"Soda?" asked Noreen.

Calliope wrinkled her nose, imagining a warm can left over from lunch in Noreen's schoolbag.

"Are you sure?" said Noreen, eyes twinkling. She lifted a square panel in the seat between them. Underneath the panel was a small door.

Calliope stared at the little door in amazement.

"Go on," coaxed Noreen, "open it."

"Okay," said Calliope, opening the door. Inside were four cans of 7UP.

Smiling, Noreen retrieved two cans, handing one to Calliope. It felt ice cold in her fingers. "Cool," Calliope said.

"TV?" asked Noreen.

"You're kidding," Calliope gurgled, dribbling soda down her shirt.

Again Noreen smiled. This time she slid back a small panel in the side of the door, revealing a set of buttons. She pushed a button and Calliope heard a mechanical hum. A small television rose out of the armrest between the two front seats.

England's Princess Margaret appeared on the TV screen. In pillbox hat and pink dress, she walked erect among a crowd of well-wishers. Every so often she nodded stiffly to someone in the crowd.

Noreen watched intently, sitting upright and nodding with Margaret.

While impressed with the TV, Calliope soon grew bored with the princess. What a stiff, she thought, and turned to look out her window.

The Mercedes was almost atop South Mountain. Calliope slipped off her seat belt, rose up on her knees and looked out the back window. Just as she suspected. You could see the skyscrapers of Manhattan shimmering on the horizon—like at the park.

Between the skyscrapers and South Mountain was a rolling green carpet speckled with houses. Calliope scanned the carpet for a speck of purple.

There, was that her house? Calliope hoped so, for she didn't like the idea of living lost in the shadow of Manhattan while Noreen lived with it head to head.

The Mercedes finally came to a stop in front of a tall iron gate that stood in the middle of a high stone wall.

Calliope had heard of these neighborhoods, where people lived walled in. At first the idea had made her laugh. She imagined people jailed inside their own neighborhood.

But now she realized she'd had it backward. Up close the gated wall looked like a raised shoulder turned against her. Like a snooty grown-up who didn't like kids.

There was a loud click and the iron gate swung

open automatically. As the Mercedes drove into the walled neighborhood, Calliope heard a nursery rhyme in her head. "Pussycat, pussycat, where have you been?"

"I've been to London to visit the queen," Calliope answered aloud.

"What?" said Noreen, looking up from the TV.

"Oh, nothing," said Calliope, giggling. Noreen looked annoyed, so Calliope tried to sit quietly and look at all the big houses they passed.

Actually it was more like a beauty pageant of houses. Each house they passed was bigger and fancier than the one before it.

There was a house with stone lions guarding a little black mailbox. Around the corner was a house with a statue of a woman out front. The woman's nose dribbled water into a scalloped bowl at her feet.

Next came a house with a large, shallow pool in the front yard. Shimmering in the blue water was a reflection of the house. The reflection made the house look twice as big as it really was.

This was some contest, but which house was the winner? It didn't take long to find out.

No Monkey Business

The Mercedes pulled into a half-moon driveway paved in bloodred cobblestones and stopped. Calliope looked up at the towering redbrick house. There were miniature towers on either corner of the front, just like a castle.

"Wow," said Calliope, throwing open the door of the Mercedes. She ran up to the house and stopped at a forbidding wooden front door.

Calliope felt someone grab her elbow and turned to see Noreen at her side.

"No monkey business, all right?" whispered Noreen.

"Monkey business?"

"You know, Barbie heads, fangs and nose harps,"

explained Noreen. "Keep that stuff in your pocket—at least until we're past Mother."

Calliope shrugged. "Whatever."

"And another thing," said Noreen, "don't speak unless you're spoken to."

Now, that was going too far. Calliope's disapproval must have shown on her face, for Noreen shook the elbow and said, "Just do it, okay?"

"Okay, okay." Noreen's house was beginning to sound like school.

Noreen smiled and looped her arm through Calliope's.

In a moment the high door opened and in the doorway stood a woman in a black dress and white lace apron.

"Miss," the woman said to Noreen, who nodded in acknowledgment.

Calliope and Noreen stepped into an eight-sided foyer. On each wall hung a painted portrait of a man or woman. Everyone in the paintings had a long nose and frowned down at Calliope.

At first Calliope tried to stare back but she was badly outnumbered. She lowered her gaze in surrender and studied the floor instead. It was quite interesting, really. There was a little red heart in the middle of every white marble tile.

First there was the red Mercedes. Then the red

house with the red driveway. And now these red-hearted tiles. Had she entered the palace of the queen of hearts?

"Off with her head."

Calliope jumped at the sound of the voice. "What?" she screeched, touching her neck.

"I said, 'Off with your shoes.' " It was only Noreen.

"Oh." Calliope sighed in relief.

"What did you think I said?" said Noreen as she stooped to unbuckle her shiny black leather shoes.

"Never mind," said Calliope, and looked down at her feet. "Oops." She'd jumped out of the Mercedes without her shoes.

She turned and ran back out the front door and onto the driveway. The Mercedes was no longer out front. She ran to either end of the half-moon drive-way but couldn't find the car. In frustration she plopped down cross-legged in the middle of the driveway.

"Looking for these?"

Calliope turned to see Charles. He held her Keds out in front of him.

"Thank you, Charles," she said, taking her shoes.

Charles nodded slightly.

Calliope ran back inside the foyer and found Noreen waiting, hands on hips. "I told you, no monkey business," said Noreen.

"Sorry," said Calliope, holding up her shoes. "I forgot these."

Noreen shook her head as Calliope handed her shoes to the maid.

"Come on," said Noreen, and headed toward one of the three hallways that branched off from the foyer.

Calliope hesitated for a moment. A little voice inside told her to check the bottoms of her feet. She raised a foot quickly. Just as she feared. Her sole was black with grime from running on the driveway. Oh, well.

Calliope followed Noreen to the hallway and then stopped. Gleaming white carpet covered the floor.

"What now?" said Noreen.

"Isn't there another way?"

Noreen scowled.

"All right, I'm coming," said Calliope, and began tiptoeing down the hall. Still, she could feel her grimy feet sticking to the white carpet.

She frowned and looked over her shoulder. Behind her trailed a faint line of gray footprints. One way or another, she was going to leave her mark at Noreen's.

The Queen of Hearts

The carpeted hallway ended at a cavernous room. Here Noreen stopped in the doorway and stood as if waiting to be called.

Calliope peered into the room. What first caught her eye was a large Oriental rug. It was red, of course.

Centered on the rug was a low table, around which sat three chairs. Two chairs were on one side of the table and a high wooden one cushioned in red velvet sat on the other.

In the high chair sat a willowy woman dressed in a black skirt, shiny black high-heeled shoes and a red blouse. She fingered a pearl necklace while gazing ahead.

"Who's that?" Calliope asked Noreen.

"That's Mother."

"It's your mom? What's she doing home in the middle of the day?"

"Shhh," said Noreen, and stood in the doorway as if waiting to be called.

Calliope stared at Noreen's mother as if she'd found an animal thought to be extinct. You didn't see many mothers home during the day in Calliope's neighborhood. Unless they were old like Mrs. B.

In a moment Noreen's mother turned to look at her daughter and smiled faintly. "Reenie," she said, beckoning Noreen with a bony hand. "There you are."

Now Noreen entered the room and walked to her mother, holding Calliope's hand.

"And this must be your little friend, Cal-*lee*-o-pee?"

Noreen didn't tell her mother that she'd mispronounced Calliope's name. Calliope was about to say something but Noreen gave her a hard look.

"Please, sit down," said Noreen's mother, pointing to the small chairs on the other side of the table.

As Calliope sat, the maid in the black dress reappeared. She carried a silver tray laden with a plate of gingersnaps, a pot of tea, a sugar bowl and creamer, two glasses of milk and a cup and saucer. Her upper arm muscles quivered as she slowly lowered the tray onto the table in front of Calliope.

Calliope hungrily eyed the cookies. They were the

tiniest cookies she'd ever seen. She prepared to lunge for the gingersnaps but then thought better of it, turning to look at Noreen.

Her friend sat upright, hands folded in her lap, eyes looking at her mother.

What was Noreen waiting for? Calliope decided she'd better wait and find out. So she too sat upright in the hard wooden chair, looking at Noreen's mother.

As for Mrs. Catherwood, she watched as the maid poured tea into the flowered cup. The maid added one perfectly level teaspoon of sugar and enough cream to turn the tea a milky brown. Then she handed the cup and saucer to Noreen's mother.

Noreen's mother accepted the tea with a nod and the maid stepped aside, waiting with hands folded in front of her.

With pinky raised, Noreen's mom lifted the cup and sipped once. Her eyes closed as if considering something important. Then they opened and she said, "Perfect, Louisa, thank you."

The maid bowed and left the room.

Mrs. Catherwood took another sip of tea, sighed and then looked up at her daughter.

It was Noreen's turn to nod, which she did once. Then Noreen leaned forward, back straight, and took one tiny gingersnap. Holding the cookie between thumb and index finger, with pinky raised, she took the tiniest of bites. Not a crumb fell.

Noreen lowered her cookie and her mother again raised her cup and took a sip of tea. The cup went down and Noreen raised her cookie for another bite. Back and forth they went.

Calliope watched in amazement. Not once did Noreen nibble when her mother sipped. What timing. It reminded Calliope of jumping rope to a rhyme. Miss a beat and you tripped and fell. You had to feel down in your toes how fast and high your friends would flip the rope.

" 'Cinderella, dressed in yella,' " sang Calliope softly, " 'went upstairs and kissed a fella.' " Those were the opening lines of a rope-jumping rhyme popular at her school.

Noreen must have recognized it immediately. She turned sharply toward Calliope, missing her turn to nibble. When Noreen didn't nibble, her mother stopped, teacup balanced in midair, looking confused.

Calliope reached down, picked up a gingersnap and bit into it loudly.

At the sound of the snapping cookie Noreen's mother turned to look at Calliope. Her left eyebrow slowly arched as if to say, "Now, what do we have here?"

The Headstand

"Calliope, I'm so glad you've come to visit us today," said Mrs. Catherwood, setting down her teacup. As the cup touched the silver tray the maid reappeared. Soundlessly she picked up the tray and carried it off.

"Reenie's told me so much about you," Mrs. Catherwood continued, as if the maid were invisible.

"Reenie?" repeated Calliope, turning to smile at Noreen.

Noreen blushed ever so slightly.

Fingering her pearl necklace, Noreen's mother eyed Calliope for a long moment. It was a look that made Calliope feel like a cantaloupe her mom was squeezing for ripeness.

"Please don't take this the wrong way," Noreen's

mother began again, "but we have to be so careful about whom we let our Reenie play with. She comes from a very special family. It wouldn't do to let her play with, well, just anybody."

"Oh, I understand completely," said Calliope.

"You do?" said Noreen's mother, amused.

"Yes, I come from a very special family too," said Calliope. She glanced at Noreen, who mouthed the word "Don't."

"Indeed," said Noreen's mother, "and what family might that be?"

"The Days of Feldman Court, of course," boasted Calliope.

"I don't believe I've heard of them," said Noreen's mother.

Calliope felt a kick in the foot. She turned to see Noreen glaring at her.

Noreen's mother glanced sharply at her daughter and Noreen immediately sat up straight.

Calliope continued undeterred. "Perhaps you've heard of my brother Frederick."

Noreen's mother looked blank.

"He once ate twenty-nine egg salad sandwiches at Grunting's all-you-can-eat family buffet," explained Calliope. "Mr. Grunting finally had to put lots of pepper in Frederick's sandwiches to drive him away."

"How . . . interesting," said Noreen's mother.

Calliope nodded. "And, then, of course, there's me."

"Hmm," said Noreen's mother, "and do you eat a lot of egg salad too?"

Calliope wrinkled up her nose.

"I see," said Noreen's mother. "So what is it that's so special about you?"

Calliope thought hard. What would impress Noreen's mother? Not much, she figured. She'd have to think of something pretty terrific. In a moment it came to her and she looked Noreen's mother in the eye. "I'm the only girl in the fourth grade who can stand on her head."

"You can what?" blurted out Noreen.

"Reenie, please."

"Sorry," said Noreen, looking more worried than ever.

Noreen was probably thinking, I've never seen Calliope do a headstand. And it was true, Calliope had never done a headstand at school. But she had done one. Once. In Jonah's room.

Headstands were part of the funny exercises called yoga that Jonah did every night in his underwear. Several weeks ago, he'd had to show Calliope how to do a headstand. It had made her head feel as if it were going to explode and she had never done another. But now she figured a headstand would prove to Noreen's mother that she was indeed special.

"Here," said Calliope, standing, "I'll show you." Calliope walked clear of the coffee table. She knelt and then put the top of her head and hands on the red carpet. It felt thick and soft. If she fell this time it wouldn't hurt so much.

Calliope's head and bent arms formed a three-legged stool. She slowly raised her legs and put them atop of her bent arms. So far, so good. She felt balanced. Now for the hard part. She began to raise her legs. Her face reddened with the effort. She looked out and saw Noreen covering her eyes.

Up, up, up went Calliope's legs. As they rose, her pockets emptied, and the nose harp, Barbie head and rubber bands rained on her face. Still, Calliope didn't lose her balance. In a moment her toes pointed up at the ceiling. She'd done it!

Calliope heard a soft clapping. She smiled, looking up at Noreen. Her hands still covered her eyes, although she peered through parted fingers.

"Darling, just darling," said Noreen's mother. It was she who was clapping. "I just love her."

"You do?" said Noreen, lowering her hands.

"Yes," said Noreen's mother. "She's so . . . so entertaining."

Calliope supposed Noreen's mother was paying

her a compliment, although it felt like something you'd say about a seal trained to spin balls on its nose. Would Noreen's mother toss her a fish now?

Calliope crumpled to the ground. She was right. The carpet cushioned her fall.

Noreen's mother stopped clapping. "Now, run along, girls, and go play."

Noreen stood, bowed slightly and took Calliope by the hand. She led her back down the hallway.

Calliope shuffled behind Noreen. "I don't think your mother really likes me," she mumbled.

Noreen shrugged. "She likes you enough to let you stay."

"Gee, that makes me feel better," grumped Calliope.

Noreen stopped and draped an arm across Calliope's shoulder. "I thought your headstand was the best."

"Really?"

Noreen nodded. "Now are you ready for something really special?"

Meet Baby

Noreen led Calliope to a big airy room with blond wood furniture and lots of windows. It had bookshelves filled with strange stuff. There were shiny boxes of all colors and designs, animals carved out of different-colored stones and earthenware tea sets. Yet nowhere did Calliope see a single Barbie doll, coloring book, box of crayons or board game.

"Don't you have any toys?" asked Calliope.

Noreen shrugged. "These are my toys—at least Mom and Dad think so."

Calliope didn't know whether to be impressed or to feel sorry for Noreen. All this weird stuff was pretty cool but she couldn't imagine growing up without a box of crayons.

She scanned the bookshelves again. This time she noticed a funny little man carved out of wood. Head cocked and smiling, the man stuck out his big round stomach and arched both arms over his head. Calliope found herself wanting to rub his belly. "May I?" she asked, pointing to the little man.

Noreen nodded. Calliope picked up the little man and stroked his belly with the tips of her fingers. She'd never known wood could feel so soft. Her lips curved into a smile not unlike the little man's.

"He's called a Buddha," said Noreen.

"Hmm," purred Calliope, stroking the Buddha man. She decided he must have been what Noreen wanted to show her. "Awesome," she whispered, giving Noreen the highest compliment among kids.

Noreen laughed. "You think this junk is what I wanted to show you?"

"It isn't?" said Calliope, now feeling confused. She noticed Noreen staring at the back of the room.

Calliope turned to look too. What she saw made her drop the little Buddha.

In the corner was a tall metal cage. A gray bird sat inside on a dangling wooden rod. With head cocked sideways, the bird watched a small TV set on a stool just outside the cage.

Calliope ran up and pressed her face against the cage's bars.

The bird looked like a small parrot, but why, then, wasn't it green?

"His name is Baby," said Noreen, standing behind Calliope. "He's an African gray parrot."

"Where'd you get him?" said Calliope. "Is your dad some kind of pirate?" She imagined Noreen's father with a sword and black eye patch. She envisioned him robbing rich travelers of shiny boxes and little Buddhas.

"No," said Noreen, sounding slightly unsure.

Calliope turned to look at Noreen. "Then what is he?"

"Well, I don't know what you'd call him," said Noreen. "Father travels the world buying all this weird stuff. Then he sells it to stores in New York for a lot of money and then the stores sell the stuff to other people for even more money."

"Sounds like a pirate to me," said Calliope. She glanced back at Noreen. "Does he ever take you with him?"

"No," Noreen said with a sigh. She waved a hand dismissively at her bookshelves. "He just brings me back all this stuff."

The stuff was nice but Calliope would have preferred traveling. Judging by the faraway look in Noreen's eyes, Calliope guessed she felt the same way.

Calliope turned back to study Baby. "Does Baby talk?"

"Of course, silly."

"Well?" said Calliope, looking expectantly at Noreen.

"Well what?"

"Why isn't he talking, then?"

Noreen raised her nose. "Baby only talks when he feels like it."

"And when is that?" Calliope pressed Noreen.

"I don't know. When he does."

Well, then, thought Calliope, she would just have to make Baby feel like talking.

Darling, Just Darling

No one, not even Frederick, could resist Calliope's jiggly tongue face. She hooked a finger in either side of her mouth, stuck out a flickering tongue and rolled her eyes.

Sure enough, Baby turned to face Calliope. He cocked his head sideways and studied her.

Come on, come on, thought Calliope, say something. Her tongue was beginning to ache.

Baby granted her wish. "Darling, just darling," he said in a voice very similar to that of Noreen's mom.

Calliope's tongue dropped in exhaustion. Did this bird think she was a trained seal too?

Noreen laughed at the parrot, something Calliope doubted she'd ever do to her mom's face.

Calliope gave her a dirty look.

"Oh, come on," said Noreen, "you have to admit he's good."

"Too good," said Calliope.

"Look," said Noreen, suddenly turning serious, "can you keep a secret?"

At the word "secret" Calliope turned serious herself. "You know I can."

No sooner had Calliope spoken than Noreen tiptoed off to the door of her room. She peeked out into the hallway and then closed the door.

"Mother would kill me," said Noreen, returning to Baby's cage.

"For what?" asked Calliope.

"For this." Noreen unlatched the door of the cage. "It's the only thing Baby likes better than TV."

Baby looked at the open cage door and squawked. With a flutter he leaped at Calliope's head.

"Geez," said Calliope, ducking as Baby soared past her and out the door of his cage.

The parrot plopped onto the carpeted floor. He shook out his ruffled feathers and stretched his neck for a long moment. Then he began to waddle around the room.

To Calliope, Baby looked like a squat captain inspecting the deck of his ship, hands behind his back. Around and around the room he circled.

Finally Baby stopped at Calliope's feet. He opened

his beak and Calliope caught her breath, wondering what the parrot would say next.

Once again he surprised her.

" 'Oh my darling, oh my darling, oh my darling Clementine,' " Baby sang in a scratchy voice and slightly off-key. He sounded like Alfalfa of *The Little Rascals,* which Calliope loved to watch on Saturday morning.

There was something endearing about Alfalfa. Was it that he never gave up, no matter what? Calliope pictured Alfalfa, face wrinkled with effort and soap bubbles streaming out of his mouth, as he sang to his true love, Darla.

Was Calliope Baby's Darla? Her heart melted at the thought. She fell to her knees, threw back her head and sang along with Baby.

Noreen dropped to her knees too, but not to sing. She was doubled over with laughter.

The three of them made quite a racket, Calliope was proud to say. Unfortunately, it didn't last long.

There was a loud rap on the door. Noreen instantly stopped laughing and jumped to her feet. "It's Mother!"

Noreen lunged for Baby.

"Unhand me, you cad," Baby squawked, and fluttered up to a shelf. He ducked behind a miniature treasure chest.

Baby hid not a moment too soon, for the door of the room opened. In the doorway stood Noreen's mother, fingering her pearls. "Reenie, must the two of you play so loudly?" As she talked, her eyes swept the room. They stopped for a moment on Noreen, who folded into herself like a flower closing its petals. Noreen's mother nodded slightly and then continued her sweep of the room.

Uh-oh, Calliope remembered, Baby wasn't supposed to be free. She jumped to her feet and backed up against the cage, her body concealing its open door.

Calliope's sudden movement caught the eye of Noreen's mother. She cocked her head sideways as if she were trying to peer around Calliope and into the cage.

"Shhh," said Calliope, putting a finger to her lips. "You'll wake him."

"Wake whom?" said Noreen's mother.

"Baby," Calliope said. "I sang him to sleep with a lullaby."

Baby, of course, was anything but asleep. At the sound of his name he began to sing again.

" 'How I love ya, how I love ya, my dear old Mammy,' " Baby sang in a throaty male voice.

Calliope recognized the words with a smile. They were from one of those scratchy old records her dad had loved to play. She threw back her head, raised her arms to the ceiling and sang along with Baby.

The eyes of Noreen's mother widened. Then, smiling faintly, she tapped the fingers of one hand on the palm of the other. "You're quite the little performer, aren't you," she said, and turned and walked out the door.

Noreen jumped to her feet and closed the door behind her mother.

At the sound of the closing door Baby stopped singing. He strutted out from behind the miniature chest.

What a naughty boy, Calliope thought with a smile as she watched the strutting parrot.

After a moment Baby settled down. Perched atop the bookcase, he scratched under a wing with his beak.

Calliope couldn't take her eyes off him.

"He's the best gift my father ever gave me," Noreen said softly.

"No kidding," answered Calliope, but it wasn't Noreen's dad she was thinking of. It was her own. There was something about Baby that reminded Calliope of him. Maybe it was the singing.

Calliope pictured Dad scooping her up in his arms. He waltzed across the kitchen, crooning in her ear, " 'It had to be you. Bah, bah, bah, bah boo. It had to be you.' "

That sounded like a song Baby would sing too. Which made Calliope wonder if Dad had led her to Baby. Did he mean for Calliope to have Baby? Her legs wobbled at the thought.

Calliope pinched her arm. Wake up, you silly goose. A misty Dad looking out for her was just make-believe. Still, at this moment, Calliope would trade Noreen her entire collection of Barbie heads for Baby. But of course Noreen wouldn't trade away Baby. Who would?

No, Calliope had to dream up a way to get Noreen to share Baby with her. Calliope bowed her head in concentration.

"Are you okay?" asked Noreen, draping an arm around Calliope's shoulders.

At first Calliope didn't reply. Then she looked up, smiling. Once again her imagination had come to her rescue.

You Don't Know

"**B**aby's awesome, all right," said Calliope, "but aren't you scared?"

"What do you mean?" Noreen answered suspiciously.

"You know."

"Know what?"

Calliope laughed nervously. "You have an African gray and you don't know?" She looked out of the corner of her eye at Baby.

The parrot had stopped cleaning himself. He studied Noreen first with one eye and then with the other. "*Awk,*" Baby suddenly erupted. "You don't know, you don't know."

Oh, Baby. Never tell Noreen she doesn't know something.

Noreen shot Baby a dirty look and then grabbed Calliope by the elbow. "Know what?" she demanded.

Calliope shook her arm free from Noreen's grip. "Noreen," she said, "African grays talk like people because they are people."

"Yeah, right," scoffed Noreen.

"Oh, not like you and me," Calliope continued. "They're people from another planet."

Noreen raised an eyebrow, trying to look skeptical, but Calliope could see it twitching.

"I know it sounds crazy," said Calliope. "I didn't believe it myself. Then my brother—the one who goes to college? He brought home this science magazine. In it was a picture of an African gray. It was wearing a general's cap and a tiny blue vest and smoking a long, thin cigar. Under the picture it said, 'Fooling the earthlings has become my planet's greatest pastime.' Can you believe that?"

"No," Noreen said weakly, her lower lip quivering.

"You see," Calliope continued, "African grays are these little people from another planet pretending to be stupid birds. *But we're the stupid ones.* They go back to their planet and have a big laugh. 'Ha, ha, ha,' they say, 'we sure fooled those stupid humans.' "

Calliope turned to face Baby. "You clever little devil," she said, shaking her finger at him.

Baby looked up from his preening. "You are

97

stupid," he said in a voice not unlike the cartoon Dexter.

Noreen shuddered and walked away. Calliope's eyes followed her friend as she sat down on the edge of the bed. For a long moment, Noreen stared up at Baby. Was she trying to detect signs of alien life? Finally Noreen turned back to look at Calliope and asked, "You're kidding, right?"

Calliope scurried over to Noreen and sat down on the bed beside her. "What if we could make all the kids in class believe it was true?" she said excitedly.

"Go on," scoffed Noreen, "no one would believe you."

"Oh, no?" said Calliope, eyeing Noreen skeptically.

"I didn't believe you for a moment," Noreen protested.

"Uh-huh."

"I didn't."

"Well," drawled Calliope, "not everyone is as smart as you." She watched as Noreen raised her sharp nose ever so slightly. "Most kids," Calliope continued, "would love to believe that Baby was an alien."

Noreen nodded thoughtfully. "But do you really think you could pull it off?"

Calliope stood and imagined herself the ringmaster at a circus. Sweeping an arm toward Baby, she pronounced, "It would be my finest moment, the greatest show-and-tell of all time." She turned toward Noreen. "Of course, I couldn't do it without your help."

"Anything," said Noreen, jumping to her feet. "Just name it."

Calliope smiled. Her plan had worked. She'd persuaded Noreen to share Baby with her. Now for the next step. "Well," she said, tapping her cheek, "for starters, we'll need a black eye patch and some doll clothes."

Captain Tweakerbeak

"This," said Calliope, "is Captain Tweakerbeak."

She stood in front of her class. Baby paced on her shoulder. He wore a little blue cap, a red vest and an eye patch. Taped awkwardly to his beak was a thin cigar.

Calliope smiled proudly at Captain Tweakerbeak's cigar, a touch she had dreamed up at the last minute. It had come from a box Frederick kept hidden under his bed.

She and Noreen had spent Sunday afternoon teaching Baby how to act like an alien. He had been a willing student. In costume he'd admired himself in a mirror, cooing, "Pretty boy, pretty boy."

They'd readied Baby at Noreen's house. At first

Calliope had wondered if Noreen's mother would welcome her, given the trail of dirty footprints she'd left behind on her first visit. But when she'd returned, the footprints were gone, and Noreen's mother greeted her with a faint smile. "Sing me another silly song," she'd said. Calliope had obliged, dropping to her knee and clasping her hands together. " 'Day-O,' " she sang. " 'Daaay-O. Daylight come and me wan' go home.' " As she sang Calliope imagined herself a court jester in checkered tights and pointy shoes with bells.

After Calliope's little performance Noreen's mother had left them alone all afternoon. They'd rehearsed and rehearsed until even Baby's voice seemed a little hoarse.

Of course, Calliope wanted to be the one to show off Captain Tweakerbeak in class, but she first asked Noreen to do it. After all, it was her parrot. Calliope knew she'd done the right thing when a smiling Mrs. B. floated through her thoughts.

Calliope watched Noreen think about her offer for a moment and then decline. Turning Baby into Captain Tweakerbeak had been Calliope's idea, said Noreen, adding, "So you should have the honor of presenting Captain Tweakerbeak in class."

Calliope couldn't tell whether Noreen meant it or

didn't want to chance making a fool out of herself. Either way, Calliope didn't mind. She was delighted as she stood now before twenty craning heads. Behind her perched Mrs. Perkins on her high stool. She nodded at Calliope to continue.

"Captain," said Calliope, eyeing the parrot on her shoulder, "why don't you say hello?"

"Ahoy there, earthlings," Captain Tweakerbeak said on cue.

Everyone laughed. Everyone but Mrs. Perkins and Thomas. Mrs. Perkins didn't say anything. She just tapped her cheek.

But Thomas, who sat up front, blurted out, "That's no ship captain, just some stupid parrot."

Mrs. Perkins clapped her hands for silence.

"It's okay," Calliope said to Mrs. Perkins. "The captain can handle this."

Calliope turned so that her parrot could eyeball Thomas. Captain Tweakerbeak clucked once and then barked, "Silence, earthling."

Thomas jumped in his seat.

"Calliope," said Mrs. Perkins sharply.

"Sorry," Calliope apologized to Mrs. Perkins. But then she winked at Noreen.

Noreen nodded slightly.

Things were going better than expected, thought Calliope. Every kid eyed her and the captain with growing curiosity. If anything, Thomas's little out-burst had helped get the kids interested.

"Actually," continued Calliope, "Thomas is half right. Captain Tweakerbeak does look like a parrot. An African gray, to be precise. Of course, looks can be deceiving."

Calliope paused for effect.

"You see," she said, scanning the class, "Captain Tweakerbeak may look like a parrot and talk like a parrot but he's not a parrot."

"He's not?" said Jamie.

"No, he's not," said Calliope. She could feel the expectation rising in the room.

Calliope drew in a deep breath and then shouted, *"He's a creature from another planet."*

This time everyone jumped in their seats, including Noreen.

"All right, that's it." It was Mrs. Perkins, who hopped off her stool.

"Well, he is," insisted Calliope.

"Yeah, and I'm Jabba the Hut," said Mrs. Perkins.

Calliope stood, legs apart and hands on hips. She looked the model of defiance.

Circling Calliope, Mrs. Perkins eyed Captain Tweakerbeak. He eyed her right back, turning in circles, following the teacher.

Finally Mrs. Perkins stopped and touched the thin

cigar dangling from the captain's beak. It fell to the floor and Captain Tweakerbeak squawked, *"Sacre bleu, mon ami!"*

Mrs. Perkins smiled. "I thought you said he was from outer space."

"He is," asserted Calliope. "See? He's speaking Tweakerese."

"Sorry," chuckled Mrs. Perkins, "but that's not Tweakerese."

"It's not?" said Calliope, her voice wobbling.

"It's French."

"French?" Calliope glanced at Noreen for support, but all she could make out was the top of her friend's head. Noreen had sunk low in her seat.

"You don't know, you don't know," Captain Tweakerbeak erupted in a voice not unlike Calliope's.

"Oh, but I believe I do," said Mrs. Perkins.

I'm Innocent,
I Tell Ya

Was Calliope in trouble? She couldn't tell from Mrs. Perkins's expression. Her mouth wrinkled indecisively as if a smile and a frown were wrestling for control. At last the smile won out.

"A parrot from another planet," chuckled Mrs. Perkins. "Very funny."

"Really?" said Calliope. Her voice was strong and clear again.

Mrs. Perkins nodded. "I think it's one of your best stories. Yes, he's adorable," she continued, stroking the parrot with a finger, "but Captain Twinkletoes—"

"Tweakerbeak," Calliope corrected.

Mrs. Perkins cocked her head at Calliope.

"Sorry," Calliope mumbled.

Mrs. Perkins smiled and then continued. "It's time for the captain to shove off."

"You mean we can't keep him in class?"

Mrs. Perkins shook her head.

"Why?" said Calliope, pointing toward the class. "Everybody likes him." It was true. Kids were leaning forward on their knees to get a better look at the captain.

"I'm afraid that's the problem," said Mrs. Perkins. "He's a bit of a distraction. Why don't you take him to Mrs. Sterne for safekeeping?"

Mrs. Sterne was the principal and her name always reminded Calliope of spoiled milk.

"Mrs. Perkins?"

"Yes, Noreen," said Mrs. Perkins.

"May I go too?" asked Noreen. "He is my parrot."

"True," said Mrs. Perkins, "but I don't like the idea of the two of you wandering the halls. Besides, I think Calliope can handle this. The parrot seems to like her well enough."

Noreen glared at Calliope as if she were to blame for Mrs. Perkins's decision. Calliope shrugged as if to say she was sorry, but she really wasn't. She liked the idea of being alone with the captain, as if he really were hers.

Calliope turned to go. At the classroom door she stopped at the sound of a loud "Ahem."

It was Mrs. Perkins. "Aren't you forgetting some-thing?" she said, pointing to a small gumdrop of a cage near the door.

"Oh, right," said Calliope. She stooped, lifting the captain off her shoulder and into the cage. "I'm innocent, I tell ya, innocent," he squawked.

"Don't worry," said Calliope, whispering into what she thought was the captain's ear. "I'll get you out soon enough."

The Intercom

There was a girls' bathroom just down the hall from Mrs. Perkins's classroom. Cage banging against her thigh, Calliope scurried toward it. At the entrance, she opened the door and peered inside. "Aww! Ahoy there, earthling," shouted the captain.

No one answered.

Calliope walked into the bathroom and set down the cage. Man, the captain was heavier than he looked. She rubbed her thigh, studying the parrot.

This was the first time the two of them had been together without Noreen. Calliope wondered, if she let Captain Tweakerbeak out, would he flutter away? Or would he again climb atop her shoulder? She had to find out, so she stooped down to open the cage. This time the captain just stood, head cocked, eyeing her. Slowly she extended her left arm toward the cage.

Still the captain didn't move.

Hmm, thought Calliope, what's missing? Then it hit her. She began to sing softly. " 'Oh my darling, oh my darling, oh my darling Clementine.' "

" 'Thou art lost and gone forever, dreadful sorry, Clementine,' " sang the captain. He waddled out of the cage and up Calliope's arm. His claws pinched terribly. Calliope winced but didn't complain. In a moment the parrot was atop her shoulder.

"Good boy," she cooed to him. He softly bit her earlobe. "Stop it, that tickles," she giggled.

Slowly she rose and walked over to a mirror hanging above one of the two sinks. She studied herself. The captain had nestled into the curve between her neck and shoulder. Where he sat felt warm like the heating pad Mom put on her stomach when it hurt.

How could she ever put the captain back in his cage? But then again, what would old Pencil Lips think if she saw Calliope with a parrot on her shoulder?

Pencil Lips was the name Calliope had given the principal, Mrs. Sterne. It wasn't a nice name, but it did fit. Mrs. Sterne's most outstanding feature were lips as straight and thin as a No. 2 pencil.

Never had Calliope seen those lips smile. Come to think of it, neither had she seen them turn down. Whatever Mrs. Sterne thought was sealed tightly behind those two thin white lines she called lips.

Mrs. Sterne was not the kind of person you looked forward to meeting, especially alone. But Calliope wasn't alone, was she? Now she had a buddy. And his name was Captain Tweakerbeak. Yes, she and the captain were like Rocky and Bullwinkle or Long John Silver and Cap'n Flint.

Pencil Lips be hanged, matey. She wasn't putting the captain back in his cage.

Calliope turned from the mirror and picked up the empty cage. "Har, har, har," she said as she clumped down the hall on an imaginary wooden leg.

In no time she reached the glass foyer that served as the entrance to the school office. Usually there were two or three women sitting behind the long front counter. No one could see Pencil Lips without their permission.

But now these women had deserted their station. Pencil Lips must have been holding another one of her big meetings behind closed doors. It was the one thing she liked better than scolding children.

Oh, well, it was back to class for Calliope and the captain. She was turning to go when a flashing green light caught her eye. It came from a tall metal cabinet behind the counter. The cabinet, of course, held the school's intercom system.

Calliope crept to the end of the counter and peered down the hallway. It was empty, except for some metal folding chairs along one wall.

"Ahoy there, earthlings." Captain Tweakerbeak's voice boomed down the hallway.

No one answered the captain's greeting, which Calliope took as an invitation to check out the intercom. She walked behind the front counter and purposely banged loudly into a chair.

Still no one came running.

Calliope strode up to the metal cabinet for a closer look. What she found was a waist-high table in front of the cabinet. On the table sat a stand-up microphone.

Now, when Mrs. Sterne's guards were around, no kids were allowed near the intercom system. Only Mrs. Hogmyrtle, the principal's assistant, got to play with the intercom.

This struck Calliope as unfair. Who more than a kid could appreciate a cabinet full of dials and knobs? In the name of all kids everywhere, she grabbed the microphone.

Wouldn't you know it? Her thumb accidentally hit the button at the base of the microphone. Some lights on the intercom flashed and it hummed.

Oh, my, someone had left the intercom switched on. How thoughtful.

Attention, Earthlings

Calliope picked up the mike in both hands and thought for a moment. Then she glanced back at the parrot on her shoulder. "What if we created our own little Martian invasion?"

"*Awk!*"

"It could work." Calliope pictured everyone running from the building, hands on faces and screaming. She'd join the rush and yell louder than anyone. What fun! And, with all the excitement, no one would know it was she who had spoken into the intercom. Her plan sounded foolproof.

"Of course, I'll have to disguise my voice." Calliope scanned the desks that sat behind the counter. There was a half-finished letter sticking out of a typewriter and she grabbed it. She crumpled the paper over the mike.

Next she found the volume control on the intercom and turned it all the way up. "Ready?"

Captain Tweakerbeak hid his head under a wing.

"Don't be such a chicken."

"Bah, buck, buck," the captain clucked nervously.

"Don't you trust me?"

Captain Tweakerbeak clucked louder.

"You'll see. I know what I'm doing." With that, Calliope clicked on the mike and spoke. "Attention, earthings. Attention, earthlings."

Her voice boomed and crackled through the halls. It made her feel twenty feet tall. She stuck out her tongue at Captain Tweakerbeak and then continued.

"This is Commander Zero, leader of the Red First Squadron, Planet Mars. We have seized your school. Do not, I repeat, do not panic."

Calliope stopped, although she had plenty more to say. But she heard something annoying. She cocked her head like Captain Tweakerbeak and listened.

What she heard was this: " 'Oh my darling, oh my darling, oh my darling Clementine.' " The words boomed and crackled through the school.

Calliope glanced up sharply. There stood Captain Tweakerbeak, his head tossed back and beak open.

"You're ruining everything," she shouted at him.

Her words boomed through the school. "Uh-oh." Calliope released the microphone button.

The microphone went dead and so did the feeling in Calliope's right shoulder. It was as if Captain Tweakerbeak had dug in his talons. "Stop it, will ya?" she said to him.

Wait a minute. Wasn't the captain on her *left* shoulder? Calliope turned to look and saw the bony fingers of old Pencil Lips.

"Having fun, are we?" asked Mrs. Sterne.

What Are You In For?

With Mrs. Sterne, punishment was never swift. She made you wait for the blow, wondering when it would fall and how. It was like waiting all day for Thanksgiving supper, only to be served a rotten egg instead of turkey.

At least Calliope didn't have to wait alone. She still had the captain, who dozed on her left shoulder. "This is all your fault," she muttered, awakening the parrot.

"Having fun, are we?" replied Captain Tweaker-beak.

"Oh, shut up."

Calliope meant to sound angry but her words came out almost in a laugh. She was in deep trouble, all right, but she felt ecstatic. Not once had Captain

Tweakerbeak tried to fly away. Not even when Mrs. Sterne had tried to remove him.

Captain Tweakerbeak had dug his claws into Calliope's shoulder and barked like a dog. Mrs. Sterne had thrown up her hands and pointed to one of several chairs lining the hall outside her office. And there Calliope had sat through the afternoon.

Calliope glanced at Captain Tweakerbeak. The parrot had been perched on her shoulder so long now that he seemed almost part of her, like a second head. The captain must have felt comfortable too, for he had dozed off again.

It was deathly still in the hallway and Calliope began to imagine what would happen if old Pencil Lips called her mom, or worse, Mrs. B. Good grief, the apologizing she'd have to do. The thought of it made her ill.

Get a grip, she told herself. What she needed was a distraction. Luckily, one came walking down the hallway in the form of a boy. He didn't seem to notice Calliope but sat down in the chair next to her. With a sigh, he sagged forward, staring at the floor.

"What are you in for?" Calliope asked him.

Without looking up, the boy said, "Spitballs." He raised his hand, which held a straw.

"Shouldn't you get rid of the evidence?"

The boy drew the straw to his chest. "You?" he asked Calliope, still staring at the floor.

"Leading an alien invasion."

The boy slowly raised his head, his eyes widening at the sight of Captain Tweakerbeak.

As for the captain, he opened one eye and studied the boy and his chewed straw for a moment. Then he barked, "What a maroon."

The boy jumped up at the sound of Captain Tweakerbeak's voice, dropping his straw. He rose to flee but stopped at a loud creak.

He turned to watch the door of the principal's office open at the end of the hall. Mrs. Sterne stood beside a weepy boy in the doorway.

"Heh, heh, heh," Captain Tweakerbeak snickered.

Mrs. Sterne's head turned toward Captain Tweakerbeak's voice. "Not that parrot again!"

Mrs. Sterne strode up to Calliope. "I'm ready for you now," she said, pointing to the open door of her office.

Calliope stood and slowly followed Mrs. Sterne. The boy with the straw nodded solemnly to her as if she were on the way to the gallows.

Laughing
Pencil Lips

"**I**'m so ashamed." Calliope sat, face in hands, whimpering. She stopped for a moment and peeked though her fingers up at Mrs. Sterne.

Old Pencil Lips sat behind her big wooden desk, looking down on Calliope in her little metal chair. True to form, the principal's lips were pressed together in a thin white line.

What is she hiding behind those lips? wondered Calliope. Toothless gums, a black tongue? Or, better yet, a forked tongue that flickers like a snake?

Calliope whimpered again and thought she heard an echo. It was the captain. He was whimpering too. If only Mrs. Tootone, the music teacher, could hear them now. She and the captain made quite a sorrowful duet.

Was Mrs. Sterne impressed? Calliope took another peek through her fingers. The principal was captivated, all right, but not by Calliope. No, Mrs. Sterne's eyes were locked on the captain, and for good reason.

The captain was dancing. He turned from side to side, head bobbing in time with Calliope's whimpering. It was quite a performance, good enough to make Calliope stop and watch.

She did, however, keep one eye on Mrs. Sterne. And she was glad she did so. For she swore that the left edge of Mrs. Sterne's lip twitched, if ever so slightly.

Mrs. Sterne noticed Calliope watching her and slapped a hand against her mouth. The principal coughed weakly but Calliope wasn't fooled.

There was something behind Mrs. Sterne's lips that she strained to keep hidden.

Of course, this only made Calliope more curious. Whatever Mrs. Sterne was hiding behind her lips, Calliope was determined to lure it out. The captain would be her bait.

Calliope stopped whimpering and sat up straight. "Captain, where are your manners? Say hello to Mrs. Sterne."

Captain Tweakerbeak ignored Calliope and instead whistled like a sailor.

"Captain!" Calliope scolded, but she wasn't really angry. She saw that Mrs. Sterne looked anything but offended. Was that the beginning of a smile under Mrs. Sterne's long fingers?

"You know," said Calliope, "he can sing."

Mrs. Sterne didn't answer, but Calliope would have sworn she head the principal giggle.

"It's true. Show her, Captain."

This time Captain Tweakerbeak didn't sing. He gave Mrs. Sterne a good hard look and then hopped off Calliope's shoulder.

"Hey," Calliope called after the parrot as he landed atop the big desk and waddled toward Mrs. Sterne. The principal slowly shook her head at the parrot.

But the captain ignored her. He didn't stop until he reached the edge of the desk under Mrs. Sterne's nose.

Now the captain sang. His voice quivered as if he'd really lost a true love named Clementine.

It was enough to make you cry—and that was exactly what Mrs. Sterne did. Tears streamed down her cheeks, which were ballooning with the effort to hold back whatever was inside.

Then it happened.

Mrs. Sterne's lips blew open like a punctured dam. Except it wasn't water that spewed forth.

Oh My Darling

Calliope grabbed the bottom of her chair—Mrs. Sterne laughed so hard it rattled the glass door of the office. It was as if the principal now remembered every time some kid had dropped his trousers or stuck a straw up his nose.

For a moment Calliope feared that the captain might be blown away. His little body bent backward but he hung on by digging his claws into the wooden desk. He sang into the gale of laughter that ruffled his feathers.

Calliope looked up into the wind tunnel that Mrs. Sterne's mouth had become. How wrong she had been about what hid in there. Mrs. Sterne had lots of teeth, big white ones. And her tongue was red and juicy.

Right then and there Calliope stopped thinking of Mrs. Sterne as old Pencil Lips. How could you not like someone who laughed this well?

Except Mrs. Sterne didn't seem to be enjoying herself. She clutched her sides as if in pain.

Rocking back and forth, she finally toppled off her chair. She hit the floor with a thud, which silenced her, but not for long.

Captain Tweakerbeak wouldn't let her stop laughing. He dropped to the floor by her head and continued his singing, this time in her ear.

"Please," cried Mrs. Sterne between waves of rolling laughter, "make him stop."

Calliope, of course, did no such thing. She didn't have to.

The door of the office flew open and in rushed Mrs. Hogmyrtle. She scurried about the room like a gray-haired church mouse, muttering, "Oh, dear, oh, my."

Mrs. Hogmyrtle circled the room several times and then dropped to her knees beside Mrs. Sterne.

For a moment Calliope feared that the captain had been squashed. But then she saw him emerge safely from under Mrs. Sterne's desk. He waddled up behind Mrs. Hogmyrtle and commanded, "Surrender, earthling."

Mrs. Hogmyrtle jumped to her feet, eyes darting about the room. In a moment she saw Captain Tweakerbeak and pointed a quivering finger at him. Then she screamed.

It was a piercing sound that would have sent most people fleeing. But not the captain.

Oh, no. He began barking like a dog while advancing on Mrs. Hogmyrtle.

The principal's assistant slunk backward toward a corner.

As for Mrs. Sterne, who looked on, she laughed and laughed.

What a circus, thought Calliope. In one ring you had the howling Mrs. Sterne. In the other you had a barking parrot who cornered a screaming lady.

The noise was too much even for Calliope. She stood up on her chair and put a finger in either side of her mouth. Then she whistled loud and hard.

The room fell silent. Captain Tweakerbeak, Mrs. Hogmyrtle and Mrs. Sterne turned to look up at Calliope.

"Come here, you," Calliope commanded the parrot. She dropped off the chair with a thud and then fell to her knees. She extended a pointed finger toward Captain Tweakerbeak.

The captain waddled up Calliope's finger and onto her shoulder.

Mrs. Sterne and Mrs. Hogmyrtle gawked at Calliope.

"What, you've never seen a parrot?"

The Big Decision

Mind you, Calliope wasn't a bad girl. She knew what was right. She knew she should let Mrs. Perkins scold her for using the intercom and should return the captain to Noreen.

Calliope told herself to do all this but when the dismissal bell rang a second later, her feet bolted. Out of Mrs. Sterne's office, through the front lobby and onto the sidewalk in front of the school. She scooted toward home with the parrot on her shoulder.

With every step, Calliope fretted. Would Captain Tweakerbeak fly off, or would a friend of Mom's spot her? Neither happened. Calliope found the streets empty. She had dashed out ahead of the other kids walking home. And it was too early for any adults to come home from work yet.

Still, her mind raced along with her feet. She told herself that Noreen wouldn't really mind that she had kept Captain Tweakerbeak. How could Calliope give him back? He'd saved her from old Pencil Lips. Surely Noreen would understand that, especially when Calliope described how the principal had wriggled on the floor like a fish out of water.

Besides, Noreen had plenty of other cool stuff left. There were the smiling little Buddha man and the colored boxes. And if Noreen still wanted a parrot, her father could get her another one. Calliope was sure he could. Yes, she could picture it all now. Noreen would get another parrot and she'd name it Madam Fretworthy. The Madam and Captain Tweakerbeak would become best of friends. They would have parrot tea parties, with Calliope and Noreen along as chaperones.

"What do you think?" Calliope asked the captain as if he could hear her thoughts.

The captain climbed atop Calliope's head. He spread his wings like sails in the breeze and yelled, "Full steam ahead."

"Aye-aye, Captain," said Calliope, speeding up until her red Keds became a blur.

Soon Calliope reached Mrs. B.'s walkway but she slammed on the brakes at her friend's front door. What was she doing? She couldn't bring Captain

Tweakerbeak to Mrs. B., at least not yet. Mrs. B. would grill her alive with questions she couldn't—or wouldn't want to—answer.

No, what Calliope needed first was a plan. She did an about-face and headed to her own house. She could stash Captain Tweakerbeak safely inside her room and plot her next move.

As usual, no one was home at this time of day. Calliope went to her room and locked the door, just in case Frederick or Jonah wandered in early.

"Well," she said, rolling her eyes up to look at the captain, "what do you think?"

Captain Tweakerbeak cocked his head and eyeballed the room. What he saw was a small square box with a low bed under a single window. The room's most outstanding feature was its shoeboxes, which lined every shelf and the top of a small desk. There were even shoeboxes lined up along the foot of Calliope's bed.

Every shoebox brimmed with stuff. One held greasy-feeling plastic insects. Another held a towering pile of magnifying glasses. Another held a collection of Barbie heads.

Calliope loved her room. It was her lair, the place where she could hide out from Mom and her brothers.

For the captain, though, Calliope's room wasn't

love at first sight. She could feel him dig his talons into her scalp.

He began to cluck nervously. With a squawk, he leaped off Calliope's head and landed on the floor. He waddled toward a life-sized doll scrunched in a corner.

Calliope had forgotten all about the doll, which a relative had given her years ago. But the captain seemed fascinated by it. Turning his head sideways, he studied the doll's skinny legs and ponytail. "Reenie?" he wailed after a moment.

Calliope didn't like the sound of that. Best she find something to make Captain Tweakerbeak feel at home. And fast. Luckily, she had just the thing.

She dashed into her closet and retrieved an old television the size of a bread box.

She put the TV on her bed and plugged it into a nearby outlet. The TV crackled to life.

Captain Tweakerbeak turned his head toward the TV. It boomed and crashed with the sounds of a cartoon.

"Come on," urged Calliope, patting the bed, "come on."

With a flutter, Captain Tweakerbeak leaped onto the bed and settled inches from the TV screen. Calliope could hear him thrumming happily.

That was a good sign but Calliope wasn't taking

any chances. She wanted to be sure the captain felt at home. "Wait here while I get you something to eat."

She dashed downstairs to the kitchen pantry. She grabbed a box of Cheerios and ran back to her room. Would Captain Tweakerbeak still be sitting on the bed?

She entered her room panting, almost afraid to look, but Captain Tweakerbeak hadn't budged. He sat hunkered down, head turned with one eye on the TV. On the screen Bugs Bunny stuffed dynamite in Marvin Martian's spaceship.

Calliope plopped down on the bed.

"Here," she said, pouring some Cheerios into the palm of her hand. "Try some of these." She stuck her hand under the captain's beak.

Without taking his eye off the TV, Captain Tweakerbeak flicked out his tongue and snatched a Cheerio into his mouth.

"Well?" asked Calliope impatiently.

"Why eat flies when I can have nice juicy spiders?" replied Captain Tweakerbeak.

The captain was speaking Tweakerese! Mrs. Perkins had been wrong. He had his own special language. And Calliope was beginning to understand it.

She knew, for example, that Captain Tweakerbeak's weird comment about flies and spiders meant he liked the Cheerios. And as if to prove her right, he began pecking furiously at the cereal in her hand.

Yes, Calliope thought with a smile, she and the Captain were going to be friends. She stroked his head while he gobbled up Cheerios. "No more cages for you, buddy," she said.

Just then the door of her room creaked. Uh-oh, she realized with a sickening feeling, she'd forgotten to relock her door. She looked up to see Mrs. B. standing in the doorway.

"There you are!" barked Mrs. B. She stood leaning on her cane and carrying Mortimer under an arm. "We've been looking all over for you. What are you doing home?"

At the sound of Mrs. B.'s voice Captain Tweakerbeak looked from the television to Mrs. B. "Ah . . . what's up, Doc?" he squawked.

Can I Keep Him?

Mrs. B. trained the growling head of her cane on Captain Tweakerbeak. "Hmm," she said after a long moment, "so this must be Noreen's exotic surprise."

That Mrs. B., she was a smart one. But not even she could resist the captain's charm. Mrs. B. should have been angry. Instead her voice betrayed curiosity.

Calliope hadn't intended for Mrs. B. to meet the captain so soon and unexpectedly. But she might as well introduce them. She stood, sweeping her arm toward the parrot on her bed. "This," she said, "is Captain Tweakerbeak. He's an alien from another planet."

Mrs. B. shifted the penetrating gaze of her cane to Calliope.

"I mean he's pretending to be an alien."

Mrs. B. cleared her throat loudly.

"I mean I'm pretending he's an alien," Calliope explained.

"That's better," said Mrs. B., stepping into the room. "Now, what's with the cap and vest?"

Calliope beamed. "That was my idea. Noreen and I dressed him up for show-and-tell."

"To be Captain Tweakerbeak?"

"Exactly."

"He does look the part." Mrs. B. sat down next to the captain.

The parrot turned to face her and squawked, "Ahoy there, earthling."

Mrs. B. smiled and settled Mortimer in her lap. The rabbit sniffed at the parrot, wriggling his whiskers.

"There's just one thing I don't understand," said Mrs. B., stroking Mortimer.

"Hmm?" said Calliope, gazing lovingly at the captain.

"What's he doing here?"

"Who?" said Calliope absentmindedly.

"Captain What's-his-name."

"Oh. Ummm . . ." Calliope paused for a moment, trying to think of a persuasive explanation. None came to mind. She would have to lie. She didn't like to, but this was an emergency. Mrs. B. wouldn't let her keep the captain for a moment if she knew he was stolen. "Noreen lent him to me for the evening."

"Really?" said Mrs. B., sounding slightly suspicious.

"Yes, we're having a sleepover. Aren't we?" Calliope leaned forward and scratched the captain under the chin. He raised his head, purring like a cat.

Calliope glanced up at Mrs. B., who studied the captain with narrowed eyes.

"Does your mother know about this?" asked Mrs. B.

"Oh, yes. Mom talked with Noreen's mom. Everything's cleared."

Did Mrs. B. believe Calliope? She stared at Calliope with narrowed eyes for a long moment. Calliope gave her her most open, honest I-would-never-tell-a-lie look. Finally Mrs. B. harrumphed. "I suppose it's possible. I'm sure your mother forgot to tell me but I don't care who's sleeping over, you still have to do your homework."

"Yes, ma'am," said Calliope, springing from the bed to her schoolbag. Never had she been so glad to do homework.

The Captain Meets the Days

Lying to Mrs. B. was bad enough. Calliope didn't dare try that on her mom. No, she'd have to persuade her mother to let her keep Captain Tweakerbeak. It shouldn't be as hard as it sounded.

After all, Mom was always trying to do nice things for Calliope, only most of them backfired. Like promising to take her out for ice cream and then not leaving enough time to do it.

Well, here was a chance for Mom to finally win big, at least in Calliope's eyes. She could let her daughter keep this parrot, and that would make up for a hundred missed trips to the ice cream parlor.

Yes, thought Calliope, smiling to herself as she sat on the floor of her room hunched over her spelling homework.

Mrs. B. sat on the bed above Calliope. She stroked Mortimer as she watched Calliope work. Next to Mrs. B. sat the captain, who quietly picked at Cheerios and watched the little television.

The peace was shattered by a crash downstairs.

"Good Lord," said Mrs. B., clutching her heart. "What was that?"

"Just Frederick," Calliope reassured her, not looking up from her homework. "He always throws his book bag into the living room corner."

The house quaked as Frederick bounded up the stairs in his army boots. He thundered past Calliope's door and up the set of stairs that led to his attic room.

No sooner had the house stopped shaking from Frederick when the front door opened again, this time softly, as if a cat burglar had snuck in.

The living room couch groaned in protest as someone sat on it.

"Now, who's that?" said Mrs. B., looking alarmed.

"That's Jonah," answered Calliope. "He's probably lying on the couch reading a book."

"Oh," said Mrs. B., relieved.

The next sound was a low rattling that moved up alongside the house. Calliope and Mrs. B. both recognized it immediately as Mom's car.

Mrs. B. put down Mortimer and rose from the bed. "I guess it's time for me to go."

Calliope's eyes followed Mrs. B. as she exited her room. Would Mrs. B. say anything about Captain Tweakerbeak to Mom? Calliope sucked in her breath as she listened to Mrs. B. go downstairs. She heard her greet Mom at the front door.

"Oh, hello," said Mom, surprised. Usually Calliope stayed at Mrs. B.'s until Mom came home. "Everything all right?" asked Mom, sounding faintly suspicious.

Calliope squeezed her pencil, awaiting Mrs. B.'s response.

"Just peachy," snapped Mrs. B. She obviously didn't agree with Calliope having the parrot but would she give her away?

"A tough afternoon with my daughter?" Mom asked sheepishly.

Mrs. B. snorted in response.

"That bad, huh?"

"Let's just say I've had my fill for the day. Well, I'm off."

Calliope heard Mrs. B. go out the door but she didn't relax the grip on her pencil. Would Mom come upstairs to scold her for making Mrs. B. angry? Calliope really, really hoped not.

Mom would meet Captain Tweakerbeak soon enough. But this time Calliope wanted to introduce him and not be caught off guard as she had been

with Mrs. B. She jumped to her feet, frantically trying to think of where to hide her bird.

In a moment she heard plates clanking in the
kitchen and relaxed. Mom wasn't coming to quiz
her. She was cooking dinner instead.

Well, not cooking. Mom rarely made anything
from scratch. A typical supper was a plate of
microwave-blasted spaghetti and sauce.

When the kitchen grew silent it was an unspoken
call to dinner. Calliope heard Frederick clomp back
down the stairs.

Calliope waited a moment to make sure everyone
would be seated and eating when she entered the
kitchen. Then she put Captain Tweakerbeak on her
shoulder and walked downstairs. She stopped in the
doorway of the narrow dinette.

Can We
Eat Him?

Calliope's family was squeezed in around the table, eating spaghetti.

Well, Mom wasn't exactly eating. She looked out the window as she twisted spaghetti tightly around her fork. Probably running down that long list of chores she kept just behind her eyeballs, thought Calliope.

Across from Mom, Jonah read a book as he ate. He raised a forkful of spaghetti but missed his mouth. The spaghetti fell down the loose neck of his T-shirt. "Darn," he said, dropping his fork to reach down his shirt.

Frederick snickered at his brother. He hunched over his plate, shoveling the spaghetti into his mouth.

Now was as good a time as any to introduce the

captain, Calliope thought. Smiling, she stepped into the dinette and cleared her throat.

"Everybody," she said, "I want you to meet my new friend and pet, Captain Tweakerbeak." She turned so her family could get a good look at the parrot.

Frederick lowered his fork and hungrily eyed the parrot. "Does it eat rabbits?" he asked.

"Of course not," said Calliope, although she should have expected the question. Frederick divided the world into two categories: the eaters and the eaten.

"Can *we* eat him?" Frederick asked, pointing his fork at Captain Tweakerbeak.

"No!" Calliope turned to face her mother and asked, "Isn't he wonderful?"

Mom stared, mouth open, at Captain Tweakerbeak.

Jonah, still fishing spaghetti out of his T-shirt, asked without looking up, "What's wonderful?"

Frederick nudged Jonah and pointed toward Captain Tweakerbeak with his fork.

Jonah looked up at the parrot. "An African gray. Cool."

That Jonah knew the captain was an African gray didn't surprise Calliope. He knew everything about everything. She often wondered why he bothered with college.

"A what?" said Mom.

"An African gray," said Jonah. "It's a parrot. Well, not just any parrot. The African gray is considered almost human in its intelligence. It can mimic nearly any sound or word."

On cue, Captain Tweakerbeak aped Frederick slurping spaghetti.

"See?" said Jonah, laughing.

He rested his chin in one hand and studied Captain Tweakerbeak. "There's just one thing I don't understand."

"What's that?" said Mom.

"African grays are extremely rare. You won't find them in pet stores."

"Really," said Mom, shifting her gaze to Calliope. "So where did he come from?"

"Africa, of course," said Calliope.

"I mean, how did he get here?" said Mom.

"I'm glad you asked, for Captain Tweakerbeak needs our help," Calliope said. "Yes. He's running away from a terrible home and guess what?"

"I can't imagine."

"He's decided to come live with us. Aren't we lucky to have him?"

"Lucky?" Mom asked, crossing her arms.

Mom's resistance surprised Calliope. How could

an animal lover such as Mom resist Captain Tweakerbeak?

With a little encouragement from the captain, Mom could be won over. But the parrot was strangely silent. Calliope whispered in what she thought might be his ear. "Sing your song."

Captain Tweakerbeak cocked his head to eyeball Calliope. He stared at her blankly.

"You know," said Calliope, and she hummed the tune. " 'Oh my darling, oh my darling, oh my darling, Clementine!' "

Captain Tweakerbeak listened and then threw back his head. What he sang wasn't "Clementine" but "Barnacle Bill the Sailor."

Frederick whistled and clapped but Mom's jaw dropped.

"Not that song!" scolded Calliope. Why was the captain being so difficult? You'd think he didn't want to live with Calliope.

There was a loud ring, which Calliope recognized as the wall phone behind her. She grabbed the receiver, taking the call as a welcome interruption.

"Do you have my Baby?" the caller shouted in Calliope's ear.

Where's My Baby?

"**W**hat?" answered Calliope.

"Do you have my Baby?"

"Your *baby*?" said Calliope, stalling. She recognized the voice: It was Noreen's.

"I'm sorry, but you have the wrong number," Calliope said, and hung up. She looked up to see her family staring at her. Captain Tweakerbeak was staring at her too.

The phone rang again. Calliope grabbed it before anyone else moved to answer.

"Don't hang up!" said Noreen.

Calliope held the phone away from her ear.

"You don't fool me. I know you're there."

"Oh, yeah?" Calliope blurted out.

"Aha! It is you!" Noreen exclaimed.

Calliope slammed the phone back into its cradle. "A salesman," she growled to her family.

As if to defy her, the phone rang again.

"Give me the phone," said Mom. She rose from her seat and tried to squeeze through the narrow opening between the table and wall. It was a difficult move, and Calliope beat her mother to the phone.

"What?" Calliope shouted into the receiver.

"I want my Baby."

"Well, he doesn't want you."

"Calliope, give me the phone," Mom repeated. She'd given up trying to squeeze out from behind the table and reached toward her daughter.

Calliope curled herself away from Mom's grasp. "Captain Tweakerbeak has decided to live with me," she announced to Noreen.

"You've kidnapped him," Noreen yelled loudly enough for everyone to hear.

"Have not," retorted Calliope.

"Yes, you have."

"I told you. Captain Tweakerbeak has decided to live with me," shouted Calliope.

"We'll see about that," Noreen shouted. "Mother!"

Let Noreen come, thought Calliope, but I won't

be here. She dropped the phone, grabbed the captain off her shoulder, hugged him to her chest and fled the dinette. Frederick and Jonah struggled to get up. By the time they were clear of the table, Calliope had bolted out the back door.

Run Away, Run Away

Calliope ran into the tangle of flowering bushes, vines and bamboo that Mom called a garden. Sharp leaves and branches scratched her arms and legs but she didn't care.

"Calliope," Mom called.

At the sound of her name, Calliope ducked behind a leafy bush. She peered through the leaves and saw her mom and her two brothers standing on the back steps.

"Surrender, earthlings," Captain Tweakerbeak called out from Calliope's arms.

"Shhh!" scolded Calliope, but she knew it was pointless. There was no way to stay hidden long with a jabber-mouth like Captain Tweakerbeak.

Putting the captain on her shoulder, Calliope

dropped to her hands and knees. The captain paced up and down on her shoulder as she began to crawl through the thick garden. Suddenly he squawked. Calliope stopped, straining to see in the dark thicket. Ahead hung a low, thorny vine. She'd almost crawled into it face first. "Thanks, Captain," she said, and changed direction. She zigzagged through the garden, guided by the captain, who called out like a foghorn every time he spotted danger ahead.

Calliope popped out the back end of the garden. Twigs were tangled in her thick blond hair and her face was smudged green from low-hanging leaves. Still, she smiled. She'd eluded her family . . . or had she? She heard something crashing through the garden like a bull elephant. Only one person she knew could make such a racket—Frederick.

Calliope sprang to her feet and bolted like a frightened gazelle. She ran through the narrow passageway between her house and Mrs. B.'s to Mrs. B.'s front yard. Which way should she go now? Instinctively she ran off toward the park.

"Whoa, Nelly, whoa," cried Captain Tweakerbeak. But Calliope didn't whoa. To keep from flying off, the captain nestled low between her neck and shoulder.

It was dark and scary but Calliope kept moving. She heard the *thud, thud, thud* of Frederick's army boots behind her. The sound drew closer. Frederick was surprisingly quick in his heavy boots. But not as quick as Calliope, at least in the thinking department. She wouldn't try to outrun Frederick. She'd outsmart him.

One thing about walking home from school every weekday, you learned every nook and cranny of your neighborhood. Calliope knew where to find every swing set, slide and playhouse between here and school. Now she'd string them together in a maze of obstacles. She smirked, picturing Frederick stumbling as the thick toe of his boot wedged in the loop of a croquet wicket.

Calliope veered off the sidewalk and down a driveway. She dashed through a playhouse, jumped over a low fence and zigzagged through some croquet wickets. She glanced back at Frederick. Although panting now, he continued to gain on her.

Darn. Not only was Frederick quick in his monster boots, he was nimble, too. Still, Calliope wasn't beaten yet. Ahead she saw a wading pool. She veered toward the pool and ran through it. Splashing water drenched her legs and shirt. "*Awk,* abandon ship, abandon ship," cried Captain Tweakerbeak.

But Calliope kept running. She could hear Frederick splashing through the pool. Then she heard something new. The *thud, thud, thud* of

Frederick's boots slowed to a stop. Calliope dashed behind a plastic slide and peered out at her brother. Frederick stood bent over his boots, cursing. They'd filled with water and had become too heavy to lift even for Frederick's powerful legs. He dropped to his knees and began to unlace his boots.

Calliope had seen Frederick tie and untie his boots. It took time, time enough for her to reach her favorite hideout in the park.

Reenie, Reenie

Take it from Calliope. Don't ever try to climb a tree with a parrot on your shoulder. He'll claw your skin raw and he'll squawk into your ear until it rings. "Upsidaysium, Upsidaysium," Captain Tweakerbeak had chanted as Calliope scaled her favorite tree near the park swings.

Even without the captain, it wouldn't have been an easy climb. Her drenched shoes kept slipping, her legs trembling from the hard run to the park. At last she had reached her branch, the one with a spot worn in the shape of her bottom.

Now she leaned back against the broad trunk of the tree and sighed. For the first time she felt the price of her escape. A welt throbbed on her cheek.

There was a stinging scratch on one arm and, of course, her feet and legs were soaked.

She had no idea what she'd do now. But she was thankful Frederick hadn't caught her.

"That was a close one, wasn't it, Captain . . . Captain?" Calliope suddenly realized that the parrot wasn't on her shoulder. She bolted upright, eyes probing the darkness. At last she spotted a lonely figure hunkered down on the branch just outside her reach.

"There you are," she said, relieved. "You scared the willies out of me." She extended an arm toward Captain Tweakerbeak but this time he didn't climb aboard.

"You're mad at me, aren't you?" said Calliope, squishing together her soaking toes. "Well, I don't blame you. I'm mad at me too. But, Captain, what choice did I have? That pool was the only way to shake Frederick. You understand, don't you?"

Captain Tweakerbeak was strangely silent and it made Calliope uncomfortable.

"I know," she said, withdrawing her arm. She groped in both pockets of her shorts. "Here," she said, retrieving a handful of soggy Cheerios and offering them to the captain.

Captain Tweakerbeak cocked his head to eye the

Cheerios. Then he sidled along the branch within reach of Calliope.

Calliope smiled. Did she know how to handle the captain or what? "Go on," she said, offering the Cheerios to the parrot.

Captain Tweakerbeak opened his beak but it wasn't to take a Cheerio. He nipped Calliope's finger.

"Hey," protested Calliope, her feelings more hurt than her finger. "What'd you do that for?"

"Reenie!" squawked Captain Tweakerbeak.

"Noreen! Where?" Calliope bolted upright, flinging the Cheerios away. Her eyes swept the park below. There was no Noreen. No anybody.

Calliope leaned back against the tree and frowned at Captain Tweakerbeak. Something wasn't right.

The captain eyed her right back and spit out, "Reenie, Reenie, Reenie."

"Hey," Calliope snapped back, "how should I know where Noreen is?" Which, strictly speaking, wasn't necessarily so. Now that she thought about it, Calliope could well imagine where Noreen was. She was frantically searching for her parrot, making Charles drive that big Mercedes up and down every street in Calliope's neighborhood. At least that was what Calliope would do if she were Noreen.

Calliope pictured Noreen inside the Mercedes.

Her teary-eyed face pressed against the window, Noreen's heart jumped at any flicker of movement. Each time, it turned out to be a darting cat or a leaf in the breeze, and Noreen's heart sank.

Calliope knew that feeling. It was as if your heart had turned to stone. Slowly it sank down through your body. Except your stone heart never hit bottom. It just kept sinking, sinking. Calliope's heart had sunk for months after Dad died. Yes, Calliope knew what it was like to lose something very dear.

"Reenie," moaned Captain Tweakerbeak.

"I've been a terrible best friend, haven't I, Captain?" Calliope said aloud.

Captain Tweakerbeak didn't answer but Calliope heard another sound. It was a low rumble. She peered out at the street. A big car prowled along beside the park. Was it Noreen and Charles? Calliope couldn't tell in the dark. One thing she did know for sure. If it was Noreen, she'd never find Calliope. Unless, of course, Calliope decided to come out.

Calliope
Comes Home

Amazingly, Calliope reached home without bumping into Frederick. She kept expecting him to pounce on her from some dark hedge. Surely he hadn't given up looking for her. That he might have abandoned his search left her feeling surprisingly peeved.

Calliope decided to give Frederick one last chance to catch his naughty little sister. She'd stand, Captain Tweakerbeak perched atop her shoulder, a moment longer on the sidewalk outside her house.

She imagined a soggy Frederick, teeth bared, emerging from the gloom and tackling her to the ground. She would scream loudly enough to rattle the windows of her house. Everyone would come rushing out to save her. Now it would be Frederick and not Calliope who was in trouble!

Arms crossed, foot tapping, Calliope waited for her brother to pounce. Where was he? Her eyes swept the street for him. It was then that she noticed the big car looming in her driveway. The car's red finish glistened under the streetlamp.

The Mercedes! Noreen really had come. Calliope froze. Was Noreen lying in wait inside her giant car? No, if she had been, she would have spotted Calliope by now. Noreen must be inside the house.

Calliope crept toward the Mercedes for a closer look. Behind the steering wheel slumped a capped figure. Its chest rose slowly up and down.

"Reenie!" the captain blurted out.

"Shush," said Calliope, but it was too late. The figure stirred to life. It turned to groggily eye Calliope.

"Miss Calliope," said Charles, Noreen's chauffeur. He glanced up at the captain. "And the missing parrot, too."

Calliope curtsied. "In person."

Charles smiled.

"I suppose Noreen's inside?" said Calliope, glancing toward her house.

"With her mother," Charles added.

Captain Tweakerbeak whistled, "Uh-oh."

As for Calliope, she just groaned.

Charles nodded knowingly.

For a moment Calliope was silent. Then she looked Charles in the eye. "Can I ask you a question?"

"Sure," said Charles, sitting up.

"Just how angry at me is Noreen?"

"Well . . . ," said Charles. He stroked his chin, lost in thought, trying to find a word strong enough to describe Noreen's feelings.

"That mad, huh?"

Charles nodded.

Calliope sighed deeply and let her head sag. "I'm scared," she confided to Charles.

Charles didn't reply but Calliope felt he was listening raptly.

"I mean I've never stolen so much as a candy bar," continued Calliope. "Now I've taken my best friend's parrot. I can't imagine what my mom will do to me."

"You're in a tough spot, that's for sure," Charles agreed. "Still . . ."

"I know, I know. I've got to turn myself in."

"I'm afraid so."

"Do you think Noreen will ever forgive me?" said Calliope, examining her shoelaces. My, how frayed they had become.

"I don't know," said Charles thoughtfully, "but I'll tell you what."

Calliope looked up at Charles.

"If it will help, I'll put in a good word on your behalf."

"You'd do that?"

"Sure. You don't seem like a bad kid to me."

"Gee, thanks!"

"Go on now," said Charles, nodding toward the house.

Calliope turned and began inching up her walkway.

"Good luck," Charles called after her.

Calliope waved back weakly as she mounted the steps of her front porch. At the open doorway she stopped. She stripped off her wet shoes and socks and left them outside. No need to anger Mom even more by tracking wet footprints across her carpet.

Calliope stood on the doorstep, her toes hugging it like the end of a high diving board. She couldn't bring herself to leap into what awaited her inside the living room. So she stood looking instead.

What she saw was a small living room crowded with people. Mom paced in the center, head down, phone pressed to one ear. Mrs. B. sat on the edge of Frederick's soft chair. She looked stonily ahead but her hands twisted the head of her cane back and forth, drilling a small hole in the frayed carpet.

Noreen and her mother sat alongside each other on the couch. Mrs. Catherwood glared at Mrs. Day and fingered her pearl necklace. Noreen sat erect, hands neatly folded in her lap. She gazed out the window.

Strangely, Calliope's brothers were nowhere to be seen. Were they still out looking for her? Or had they just gotten bored waiting and tromped off to Herschel's for sodas and chips?

Either way, Frederick and his ever-patrolling eyes were absent. For a blissful moment, Calliope was invisible. Then Captain Tweakerbeak opened his mouth. "*Awk,* what's up, Doc?"

The Temptation

At the sound of her Baby's voice Noreen's head turned sharply. Her eyes locked on Calliope and she leaped to her feet. "There they are!" she shouted, extending an arm like a spear pointed at Calliope's heart.

Noreen's mother looked up as if she didn't recognize her daughter.

Noreen blushed and mumbled, "Sorry." Then she marched, arms extended, toward Calliope.

"Reenie," squawked Captain Tweakerbeak, and fluttered off Calliope's shoulder and into Noreen's outstretched arms.

Noreen snuggled the parrot to her chest and glared at Calliope.

"Sorry," whispered Calliope, head bowed.

"Hah!" snorted Noreen, and turned sharply so her back was facing Calliope.

Calliope looked to her mom and Mrs. B. for sympathy but found none. Mrs. B. shook her head, clucking softly. She was probably still sore about the lie Calliope had told her.

As for Mom, her brow wrinkled at the sight of Calliope's scratches, green smudges and matted hair. She opened her mouth to speak but was cut short by Mrs. Catherwood.

"That bird," sputtered Noreen's mom, face reddening.

Noreen turned to look at her mother in surprise. You'd have thought her mom had never lost her temper. At least in front of Noreen.

"Mother, please," said Noreen. "You're making a scene."

Mrs. Catherwood simmered down a bit but she still looked vexed. Twisting her pearl necklace, she lectured her daughter. "Really, Noreen. I've had it with that bird. It's been nothing but trouble since the day your father brought it home."

"No, it hasn't," countered Noreen.

"Please," said Noreen's mom, raising a hand like a crossing guard stopping traffic. "Don't think I haven't seen that bird parading around your room. He's tearing up the carpet."

Noreen blushed.

"Now all this," said Noreen's mom, flicking her hand at Calliope. "Enough is enough." She turned to face Calliope. "Young lady, I have a proposition for you."

"A propo-what?" said Calliope, not sure if this was something good or bad.

"If you really want this parrot," said Noreen's mom, "he's yours."

"What?" croaked Noreen, clutching the captain to her chest.

Calliope bit her tongue. Otherwise she would have blurted out, "Gee, thanks." Of course she wanted the captain. Who wouldn't? But she knew now that he didn't want her. Noreen was his true love. And Calliope had almost broken his heart— and Noreen's, too—by taking him. She wasn't going to make that mistake again.

"Well?" said Mrs. Catherwood.

"That's very nice of you," said Calliope, trying not to make Noreen's mom any angrier. "But no, thanks. I've learned my lesson. The captain belongs to Noreen."

Calliope knew she'd said the right thing when she heard Noreen sigh deeply. Noreen's mom, however, was not impressed. "That's very noble, I'm sure," she snapped. "But it's either you or the petting zoo for that . . . that bird."

The petting zoo? Calliope pictured the captain perched among the long rows of scraggly birds in the zoo's aviary. It wasn't a pretty picture. The captain deserved better and so did Noreen. Calliope didn't relish challenging Mrs. Catherwood, but what choice did she have? Someone had to talk her into letting Noreen keep Captain Tweakerbeak.

"I'm sorry," said Calliope, firmly but politely. "But you can't give the captain away."

"I beg your pardon," said Noreen's mom, raising her nose and looking down on Calliope.

"I said, you can't give the captain to the zoo, to me or to anyone else."

"And why not, may I ask?"

"Because Noreen loves him. Look." Calliope pointed to Noreen, who cradled the parrot. As she gently rocked him, the captain hummed, " 'Oh my darling, oh my darling, oh my darling Clementine.' "

Calliope heard her mom's familiar sigh. Mrs. Day had lowered her phone and studied Noreen with a sad smile. Even Mrs. B., looking on, had the trace of a smile on her lips.

As for Noreen's mom, well, at first she gave her daughter a look that could freeze a warm muffin. But slowly her icy stare thawed. "Reenie," she cooed, "how would you like a nice French poodle?"

"You mean instead of Baby?" asked Noreen.

"We'll trade him in," pressed Noreen's mom.

Noreen looked hard at her mother.

"Then how about a Pekinese?"

Noreen sharply shook her head.

"Two Pekinese?"

Noreen stomped her foot and turned her back toward her mother.

"You see?" said Calliope. "They're inseparable."

Noreen's mom twisted her pearl necklace until it looked ready to snap. "Oh, all right," she blurted out. "You can keep the bird."

Noreen flipped back around, beaming.

"But he stays caged while in my house," said Noreen's mom, wagging a finger at her daughter.

"Yes, ma'am," Noreen said meekly.

Mrs. Catherwood turned sharply to face Calliope, scowling. "As for you . . ."

Calliope bowed her head, ready for the worst. There'd be no more visits to Noreen's house, she was sure of that.

Mrs. Catherwood was silent for a long moment and Calliope peeked up at her, surprised by what she saw. Not only was Noreen's mom no longer scowling, she smiled. Well, almost.

"You know," Noreen's mom began again, "there

aren't many people who can make me change my mind." She glanced at Calliope's mom. "Quite impressive."

"Yes," said Mrs. Day, "we're quite proud of our little Calliope—most of the time. Right now, however, isn't one of those times." She pointed her portable phone at Calliope. "That was Mrs. Sterne. What in the world happened at school today?"

Mrs. B. narrowed her eyes at Calliope.

"Ah . . . ," Calliope began, but the sound of thundering feet interrupted her explanation. Through the front door stumbled Jonah and Frederick. "There you are!" mumbled Jonah through a mouthful of chips. His hand clutched a soda.

Frederick stood, soggy boots in hand. His bare feet were covered in mud and grass. He looked at Calliope murderously for a moment and then lunged at her.

"Yipes!" squealed Calliope, and turned to run. She didn't get far. Frederick scooped her up in his viselike arms and pressed her to his chest. Breathless, Calliope readied herself for a crushing death. At least it was a fitting end for a theatrical girl who'd wronged her best friend and Mrs. B. and her principal, too. Then, ever so slightly, Frederick's grip loosened. Not enough for her to wriggle free, mind you. But it was enough for a stunned Calliope to see that Frederick was trying, in his own awkward way, to hug his little sister. "Man, can you run," wheezed Frederick.

Now, that was a first. Maybe Frederick really did love Calliope after all, as she had long suspected.

Calliope Does Her Time

Poof! went the chalky erasers as Calliope slapped them together. A swirling cloud of white, blue and yellow chalk dusted her from head to toe. She didn't mind, though. This was the fun part of her weeklong sentence of hard labor.

She stood just outside a rear door of the school. At her feet was a plastic bucket filled with clean erasers. Again she slapped the erasers together in her hands and wondered if there had ever been a kid who'd done so much wrong in so little time. She doubted it. Even Mrs. Sterne had seemed awed when she reviewed Calliope's rap sheet of bad behavior.

Count one: using the office intercom, an offense worthy of a major punishment in and of itself. Count two: distracting Mrs. Sterne from delivering that much-deserved scolding. Count three: leaving the principal's office without permission. Count four: leaving school early. Count five: stealing her best friend's parrot. And, separately, she'd lied to Mrs. B. about it.

Mrs. Sterne, with Mom's approval, had sentenced Calliope to clean every chalkboard and eraser on the fourth-grade hall for a week. But that wasn't all. Mom had made Calliope apologize to Mrs. Sterne, Mrs. Hogmyrtle, Mrs. Perkins, Mrs. B., Mrs. Catherwood and Noreen. Every apology had been delivered with a plate of Calliope's famous M&M sugar cookies. One bite could sweeten the foulest of bad humors.

The cookies certainly had worked on Mom. Biting into a sugary cookie, she sighed and then blamed herself for Calliope's behavior. From now on, Mom promised, she'd try to be less distracted and to spend more time with her only daughter.

Mrs. B. was not as easily impressed. "Don't try to butter me up," she mumbled through a mouthful of cookie. "If you ask me, you got off too easy."

Too easy? Calliope groaned, her chalky arms sagging with fatigue. Geez. What did Mrs. B. want? Calliope to tar the school roof?

Mrs. B. wasn't the only one who hadn't quite forgiven Calliope. Noreen had turned her nose up at

Calliope's plate of cookies and given them away to Thomas. Of all people! Then she'd asked to have her seat moved away from Calliope's. Mrs. Perkins obliged, reseating Noreen on the other side of the class. But that wasn't what really hurt.

What really hurt was this: at recess, with Noreen again ump, Calliope had run home after she'd been tagged out at third base. Everyone saw it but Noreen preferred to give Calliope the run rather than to argue about it.

Bang! Calliope slapped together the last dirty erasers. Then she put them in the bucket and carried it back inside the school. Down the fourth-grade hall she trudged, bucket swaying. At each classroom she stopped, dropped off two erasers and then chatted with the teacher. She could have been a friendly mailwoman working her neighorhood route.

Calliope's classroom was the last stop. Inside, Mrs. Perkins hunched at her desk, grading yesterday's spelling test. "How'd I do?" asked Calliope, walking up behind Mrs. Perkins and peering over her shoulder.

Mrs. Perkins raised her head, frowning at the interruption. Or pretending to frown, thought Calliope, for Mrs. Perkins's eyes twinkled.

For a moment Mrs. Perkins quietly studied

Calliope. Then she shuffled through the papers on the desk. At last she held up a test with a big red A+ in crayon. It was Calliope's paper.

"Yes!" said Calliope, slapping her knee. She put down her bucket and skipped out of the classroom. A moment later she returned with a damp cloth. She dragged Mrs. Perkins's stool to the chalkboard and climbed atop it.

"You know," said Mrs. Perkins, tapping her temple with the red crayon, "I've been thinking. How would you like to come back next week after school every day?"

And clean chalkboards and erasers? "No, thanks," said Calliope as she wiped the day's vocabulary list from the top of the chalkboard.

"Not as punishment," said Mrs. Perkins, "but as my assistant." She pronounced "assistant" as if it were an important position.

Still, Calliope was suspicious. She stopped wiping and turned to face Mrs. Perkins. "What does an assistant do?"

"Well," said Mrs. Perkins, pausing as if she were dreaming up the job on the spot. "I guess your main job would be to keep me company."

"Doing what?"

"You could sit and talk to me while I work."

"Really?"

Mrs. Perkins nodded.

Calliope weighed Mrs. Perkins's offer. How many kids get to be friends with the teacher? Then again, it would mean giving up snacking on Cheerios and orange juice with Mortimer and Mrs. B.

"I'll tell you what," said Mrs. Perkins, rising from her desk. "You think on it for a minute while I go to the office."

"Okay," said Calliope, watching Mrs. Perkins depart. Truth was, Calliope already knew her answer. No way was she giving up her afternoons with Mrs. B., even if Mrs. B. was still peeved at Calliope.

Calliope resumed cleaning the chalkboard. As she struggled to reach the upper corners, she thought about Noreen. Would she ever be able to wipe the slate clean with her friend? Before she could reach the farthest corner, Calliope froze. She could have sworn someone was watching her.

Why'd You Do It?

Calliope turned to look at the doorway. There stood Noreen, a cloth as white as fresh snow in her hand. Eyes fixed ahead on the chalkboard, Noreen didn't speak. She glided silently up beside Calliope and began wiping down the chalkboard. Her cloth rotated in small precise circles that erased chalk without raising a speck of dust.

Hands on hips, Calliope stared at her friend. Not once, however, did Noreen turn to look at Calliope.

How strange, thought Calliope. It was as if Noreen wanted to be friends yet couldn't quite bring herself to make up. Calliope would have to nudge her the rest of the way. But how?

As she watched Noreen's precisely circling hand, Calliope had an idea. What if she turned cleaning the chalkboard into a game? She raised her cloth, pressed it to the chalkboard and began circling in unison with Noreen.

At first Noreen pretended not to notice. Head bowed in concentration, she just kept cleaning. But Calliope caught Noreen's eyes drifting sideways, spying on the hand moving in time with her own. With a flick of her ponytail, Noreen accelerated her circling hand.

Calliope, of course, kept pace.

Noreen shot Calliope a look that said, "Oh yeah? Try this!" Her precise circles widened into big sweeping O's.

Calliope aped Noreen but she had to stand on her tiptoes to do it. Noreen had longer arms and the top of her sweeping O's nearly touched the top of the chalkboard.

When Noreen saw Calliope imitating her sweeping O's she began inching down the chalkboard. Calliope followed. Faster and faster, like a scurrying crab, Noreen sidled—until she sidled right off the end of the chalkboard and banged into the corner of the classroom. Noreen fell backward, a soft *"Oof"* popping out of her circle of a mouth as she hit the floor bottom-first.

Calliope tried not to laugh. Standing over Noreen, she offered a chalky hand up.

At first Noreen crossed her arms and gave her ponytail a sharp flip. But she didn't stay angry long. Giggles began bubbling up through her like a freshly opened bottle of soda. Noreen took Calliope's hand and stood up.

Once standing, Noreen grew solemn again. Staring down at her shiny black shoes, she mumbled something.

"Huh?" said Calliope, cupping a hand to her ear.

"I said, 'Thank you.' "

"For what?" said Calliope. "I should be the one doing the thanking around here. You helped me clean my last chalkboard. My punishment is over."

"Oh, no," countered Noreen, looking up at Calliope and staring her square in the eye. "I'm the one who should be saying thanks. You talked Mother into letting me keep Captain Tweakerbeak."

"No, I owe you," Calliope insisted.

Look at the two of us, thought Calliope. Hands on hips, brows furrowed and arguing again. That must mean we've made up. But this time Calliope didn't feel like fighting, at least not right now. "Let's not argue," she said, lowering her arms.

"Okay," agreed Noreen, lowering her arms too. She studied her friend for a long moment.

"What?" said Calliope, uncomfortable under Noreen's questioning gaze.

"I have to ask you something," Noreen said.

"Okay," Calliope said hesitantly.

"Why did you take the captain?"

Calliope blushed. "Oh, that."

"Yes, that," said Noreen pointedly.

"I'll tell you on one condition. You have to promise not to laugh."

Noreen eyed Calliope again for a long moment and then said, "Well . . . okay."

"Pinky shake that you won't," said Calliope, thrusting a pinky into Noreen's face.

Noreen raised her nose, looking down on Calliope's pinky.

"Well?" said Calliope, shaking her pinky under Noreen's raised nose.

"Well . . . all right." Noreen hooked her pinky around Calliope's.

Pinky entwined, Calliope began to explain. "Sometimes I like to pretend that my dad is watching over me."

"Like an angel?" said Noreen.

"No," Calliope said thoughtfully, "I think more like a ghost."

Noreen's lower lip quivered.

"Not a scary ghost, mind you," said Calliope. "Just

one who looks out for me. Like saving me the last ice cream cone in the cafeteria at lunch."

"Okay," said Noreen impatiently. "But what does your dad have to do with the captain?"

"Well," continued Calliope, "when I met the captain, I thought, He's the kind of pet Dad would have given me."

Noreen still looked confused.

"I began to think that the captain was meant for me—that my dad wanted me to have him."

Noreen lowered her nose, her sharp look of inquiry softening.

"But once I had the captain he didn't want me," said Calliope. "He only wanted you and that made me feel how much I miss my dad—and how much you must be missing the captain."

"Oh, Calliope," said Noreen. "That's so sad." She dropped Calliope's pinky and embraced her instead. Calliope hugged her in return.

"Well," said a voice that came from the doorway.

Calliope turned her head and saw Mrs. Perkins.

From the doorway Mrs. Perkins studied the girls with a half smile. Addressing Noreen, she said, "I suppose I'll be moving your seat *again.*"

"Yes, ma'am," said Noreen, slipping free of Calliope's embrace. "If you please."

Mrs. Perkins grinned at Noreen.

"What?" said Noreen, and then looked down at herself. There was a chalky, multicolored outline of Calliope imprinted on her white blouse and black skirt.

Having Fun Yet?

"**H**old still," fussed Noreen as she struggled to tape a slender cigar onto the beak of her parrot. She sat in the middle of the floor of Calliope's bedroom, barefoot, her bare legs crossed Indian style. In front of Noreen the parrot, dressed in eye patch, cap and vest, rocked from side to side as if anxiously waiting to go onstage. "Ta-da," said Noreen, finally securing the cigar. "The captain is ready for his next adventure."

"Huh?" said Calliope, who sat barefoot and cross-legged opposite Noreen. Her eyes were focused not on the captain but on the bottom of Noreen's feet. How pink they were, and unscratched. Had Noreen never run barefoot through her backyard? Boy, she had a lot to learn about being a kid.

"Okay," said Calliope, looking up expectantly at Noreen. "Now, what should we pretend?"

"Don't look at me," said Noreen. "That's your department."

The captain pecked Noreen's leg and then looked up at her, clucking impatiently.

"Come on, now," teased Calliope, "the Captain's waiting."

"Okay, okay," grumped Noreen. She stroked her chin, looking up as if an idea for a good adventure were written on Calliope's ceiling. "I know," she said, eyes brightening. "We could pretend that he's Commander Zero, leader of the Red First Squadron, Planet Mars."

"Ha, ha, very funny," said Calliope. "Now try and think up something original."

"That's not fair," said Noreen, flicking her ponytail.

"What's not?"

"How come when you thought up Commander Zero it was original but when I think him up, it's not?"

"Oh no you don't," said Calliope, shaking a finger at Noreen. "You can't confuse me. Now, look at the captain and open your mind. What do you see?"

Raising her nose ever so slightly, Noreen looked

down on the parrot. She watched him pace back and forth with his eye patch and cigar. "Well, he looks mad."

"He's probably fed up waiting for his adventure to begin," chided Calliope.

Noreen shot Calliope a withering look but then her eyes suddenly flashed. "Oh my gosh, I've got one."

"An idea?"

"Yes," said Noreen, flapping her hands in excitement.

"Well, what is it?"

Noreen calmed herself. She sat up straight and raised her chin.

"Well?" said Calliope impatiently.

"The title of my adventure," Noreen announced as if presenting a report in front of the class, "is 'Captain Tweakerbeak's Revenge'."

Calliope's jaw dropped. What a great title! She wished she had thought of it herself. "What's it about?" she eagerly inquired.

Noreen began hesitantly, clearly making the story up as she went along. "Captain Tweakerbeak returns to Earth. He's back to punish the one who punished his first mate, Calliope Day."

"Go on, go on," urged Calliope.

"The captain captures Mrs. Sterne," continued Noreen, gaining confidence. "He takes her back to his spaceship and ties her to a chair."

Calliope clapped excitedly.

Noreen paused, flashed Calliope a wicked grin, and then continued. "Mrs. Sterne's eyes widen in horror when she sees what Captain Tweakerbeak holds under his wing—"

"What, what?" Calliope interrupted.

Noreen arched an eyebrow.

"Sor . . . ry," said Calliope.

"As I was saying," continued Noreen, feigning irritation, "the captain holds under his wing a feather the size of a broomstick."

That did it. Calliope couldn't control herself another second. She plunged into Noreen's story. "He raises the feather . . ."

"And sticks it under Mrs. Sterne's armpit," added Noreen, "and begins tickling her. . . ."

"Mrs. Sterne starts to laugh and laugh," continued Calliope.

"She laughs so hard . . . ," said Noreen.

". . . That her thin pencilly lips get stuck—in a grin," said Calliope.

"Yes," said Noreen with finality, "from that day on, the only face Mrs. Sterne can make is a smile."

The idea of Mrs. Sterne smiling against her will

was too much for Calliope and Noreen. They exploded in laughter, toppling to the floor. Around and around the two girls rolled like marbles. Eyes blurred with tears, Calliope looked at the captain.

Head aslant, the captain stared back with a look of mild disgust. *"Awk,"* he said, not unlike Mrs. Sterne, "having fun, are we?"

About the
Author

Charles Haddad is a journalist working for *Business Week*. He was thrilled to revisit Calliope and her family in his second novel. This story, like *Meet Calliope Day*, is set in Haddad's hometown, South Orange, New Jersey. Haddad attended Sarah Lawrence College and Harvard University. He lives in suburban Atlanta with his wife, Susan, and their son, Matthew.